TEQUILA SUNRISE

Caroline Clemens

Tequila Sunrise

I dedicate this novel to my mother,
Marilyn Jean Liphart Clemens,
mother of five and
owner of Sun Travel Service in Huron, Ohio.
Thanks Mom!

Table of Contents

Prologue

Tequila Sunrise is the fourth novel in the coastal thriller series. It follows Three King Mackerel and a Mahi Mahi as the first, Magenta Fleurs as the second, and Ballyhoo being the third. All can be read alone or in order as the characters fluctuate and regroup solving crimes and other disasters like Mother Nature. Do I qualify to write about a hurricane? Yes, I do.

In fact, I have been through three now, with two going directly overhead in the same season as the eye passed directly overhead. I waited one of those out in a bathtub with pillows, scared to death, shaky, and glad to be alive when it finished its business. Numerous tornadoes touched down but I was unscathed. I am a writer, of course there was a mishap. The truth is I lost my 25K words, or a third done manuscript after the third hurricane. We lost power for five days, and maybe I did not save it properly, but when power returned it was gone. It took me seven months to get back working on the script. This novel is a work of fiction.

I hope you never go through a hurricane except for this story. Light a candle, make a drink, turn the lights down and set the ceiling fan on low for some wind. You might feel like you are on some ship out to sea reading by candle light and swaying with the boat. Experience a hurricane in your kitchen or wherever you read while learning about Rachel, Rocco, boys Henry and Patrick, and a hurricane named Rebekah made by Mother Nature.

—Caroline Clemens

1

Rebekah Turns

"Seth, what a nice surprise to hear your voice," Rachel rambled.

"Rachel, good to hear your voice as well. Let us catch up real soon. I wanted to make sure you knew the hurricane turned inward sooner than expected."

"No, I did not know that. Patrick and Henry are watching Xochi while I get my last supplies."

Rachel turned the radio on in her car and quickly assessed her plans. She had decided to go to the store today, even though she had made sure she had about everything she needed. If the storm came closer to her, power may be out for longer than expected. She wondered if she should leave the island voluntarily, or if they would make everyone go inland to safety. Damn. Stay calm she told herself. Her house was newer, built sturdy to withstand high winds and storms. Her house was not actually hers but a friend who went abroad for a couple years and insisted she live in it while she was gone.

Rachel found a news station on the radio to catch the latest report. She mentally made a plan to get in and out of the store with supplies, return home to the beach house, and unload and find a television station to track the storm. No need to panic this soon she told herself. She had time. The beach house was not a house but rather a mansion. Her friend, a millionairess due to her father's company wanted her to live in it. She wanted to help Rachel get on her feet after adopting her sister's kid. Her friend felt compelled to help because she had been given so much to her in life. Rachel accepted and the rest is history. She would live in the house about two to three years, save money for her own home, and then settle somewhere with a good high school for Patrick. She had a plan and she had time.

Her and Seth had broken off their reunion from the sailboat adventure or drug bust to put it more accurately. That was some adventure. It was thrilling being on a sail boat looking for fentanyl hidden by cartels and other bad persons. But the hurricane category one that came through while she was at the helm was a nightmare she had not planned on. However, she survived. That would never happen again. Right? Girl, wake up! You live in Florida and hurricanes come every year. Would she ever get used to them? Think about that next week she told herself when this one named Rebekah passed on through.

She parked the car and hurried into the store pulling out her penciled list she had made yesterday. She told herself to buy some canned goods in case the power went out for more than twenty-four hours. The boys would be fine living on peanut butter and bread for sure. Maybe though, she would come up with something more fun for camping post hurricane. Beef jerky and water crossed her mind. The store had a steady stream of local patrons doing exactly what she was doing. Stockpiling. She could look at another's cart and add to her list with things like paper towels and toilet paper. Rachel wondered does the plumbing even work in a disaster? She answered her own question. It must.

The tempo all around her picked up the pace as she returned to her car. The streets seemed busier with more traffic going both ways. She must get home and turn on the news and unpack her supplies. She gave more thought to the Category One hurricane out at sea earlier this summer and when one does not know it can help by not getting worked up. She thought about Seth. She had taken the kids to visit him as he was a big part of their lives. The dramatic change which occurred in him was stunning. She hoped he did well in getting on with his new life. Once she was in the driveway her thoughts turned elsewhere. Her own life had a new beginning of sorts. She had been brave and made a big change herself. Did the sailboat cause or stir a change in both? Was it timing? Maybe it was trauma. She had learned trauma can propel you forward or sink you to lower depths for a while. She had no time to ponder any depths as she had a child now. And that was paramount. It superseded everything else.

She made a quick note to herself to call the boys once she had the supplies in the house. It took three trips back and forth from car to the kitchen. Why so much she asked herself? Just in case the power went out and she had two boys to feed. Xochiquetzal was going to stay with Henry's mom while Henry was staying with Patrick and her. The moms thought it best for the week that the storm came. The distance was only about four miles on the outer island with a bridge in between them. Rachel found the remote and turned on the news for weather updates while she put away the extra groceries and supplies. The kitchen was expansive with a white granite counter and large singular iron pendants for light. The wooden table sat in front of the window which held views of the path to the ocean and the ocean itself off in the distance. This house was set back from the ocean and she guessed that might make it better during a storm. She was sure of it.

She turned on the crystal chandelier over the dark wooden table and imagined a family sitting around here chatting and discussing the tales of the day with warmth, fervor, and love. Maybe she would have such a family. She smiled and continued making sure her list was updated for the coming hurricane. She poured herself a glass of wine and took it and herself to the master bedroom and bath. The boys would not be home until seven but well before dark. This is her time to relax before the storm. She lit a candle and filled the bathtub up with warm water. She told herself to make a dinner using the oven tonight, just in case the power goes out two days from now. She turned her phone on for her musical playlist, which she had just begun to make. Rachel had about fourteen songs which she kept on repeat but would add more soon.

Lately she was listening to a new girl sing about coffee and new beginnings. She played those songs, sipped her wine, and forgot about the coming hurricane. It was then her focus shifted to the new job offer from a man, rather her future boss, whom she had just met. He had offered her a new job.

She would be leaving the hospital for a brand-new adventure filled with excitement, and thrills. Thrills as in saving lives every week and being in full control, not controlled by others. The last three weeks had been the best. She had new tunes she listened to on the radio, and a new job offer. Her mind lingered on this guy as she meandered over and over the last few weeks and all their meetings. She had never heard of him before. Ever. He had just appeared out of nowhere and surprised her. Quite a nice surprise. He was in a similar field like her and their paths had crossed. Collided. Her future looked brighter than ever even with her and Seth parting ways. Maybe they never were to make it all the way. She would be friendly and he would likely give her a significant discount on a good piece of art or a special painting from one of his students. When she bought her new house, she would need that sort of thing she thought.

She closed her eyes and relaxed in the tub. Twas the calm before the storm and her home, a mansion, would withstand a little old hurricane. Of course, it would. She made another mental note to add to her list. Do laundry in case there is no power and the water is shut off or something. The house came with a piano so she would have music, even if she had to play a song herself. She chuckled. Relax in the bath, might be your last for a while. Her thoughts went to him, the new guy with dark hair, dark eyes, a beard, and a mustache. In all her life she had never kissed a man with a mustache or beard. Was she missing out? Maybe. These thoughts were consuming her and she did not mind. She guessed it was the first time she was alone without the kids and not being at work in either job gave her a moment to herself. She smiled and turned the music up, a jazzy piano tune played. She sipped more wine and drifted off to a place she did not know existed. This place had no worries of a hurricane and the sandy beach welcoming the ocean swells made for a good feeling about life.

Rachel was set in a good place. Things were happening and all of it seemed to be coming together like it was meant to be. She loved being a mom. Nursing was exciting and a new job would put her at the top of her league skills wise. She finished her bath and dressed in a robe then made way for the kitchen. Cook some food for the week she told herself. As she did this she wondered where the boys were. She checked her phone. Ah ha, there was a text message from Patrick. She read it, then read it again.

Patrick: Mom, we went to Nates place to hang out before the storm. We will come back tomorrow as it is getting dark. Okay? Henry and I did the chores list you left. You're welcome!

Rachel: Okay. Love you sugar. Stay safe. (she kissed the phone).

Patrick: <3

2

Three Weeks Prior

Three weeks prior to the approaching hurricane named Rebekah, Rachel was enrolled in a helicopter course to become a helicopter rescue nurse, or flight nurse. She could not believe her lucky stars as this was something she always wanted to do. It was her turn to shine her little boy told her. She blessed her sister at that moment because she had not been around Patrick long enough for him to have picked up something as wonderful from her as that comment.

Today was the first day of a five-day course to become a nurse who flies in copters and rescues injured persons anywhere but especially remote areas including highways, waterways, boating, or lake accidents. Her experience in the hospitals would greatly help with the patient to nurse contact, and this course would give her the time elements that she would have to factor in for patient safety and timely arrivals to centers of care.

Rachel received an email from a friend after telling her she was going to investigate helicopter rescue nursing. She signed up for the course immediately. They had an opening and here she was. Day one should be fun. Meanwhile, she hired a sitter for Henry and Xochi for the week. She did not want to worry about the boys sneaking out in the boat going somewhere new for thrills. Her mind was at peace and she was prepared to learn new material. She had been told she would even learn to fly the helicopter for a short distance for emergency use in case of pilot failure. Pilot failure, well, she had never thought of that. Good God, would she have to be a pilot as well? She shook her head. I am sure they have this all figured out. The first three days were at the local airport and the final two days over near the beach at a remote airport. She knew Henry would absolutely grill her about every detail when she got home.

Rachel and three other nurses, all ICU trained, showed up for the five-day class. They had their coffee and were instructed to report to a conference room. Half of today would be class indoors and then this afternoon a ride out over the ocean and selected highways to view. The instructor presented a short video about helicopter rescues referring to this helicopter as an ICU in the sky. The class knew this was a step up from any bedside hospital care and that care and recovery along with timing were key elements in saving a life, or maybe two if it was a pregnancy or car crash.

Momentarily, after the video, Rachel thought to herself she might quit her extra job and devote the extra time to this new venture or more time for Patrick. It is funny how those small changes creep in at different times in our life, almost as if your brain knows your busy so it stirs you and inoculates the desire to set in motion. Maybe this job will bring other changes into her life. For the rest of the morning the crew inside this conference room took detailed notes about what they would be doing inside the airborne helicopter. For two days they would be following this pattern, then on Wednesday more note taking for specific situations with death imminent unless cared for and quickly. Thursday would be a review of all the material, the information and instruction, followed by more tours in the helicopter with landings and takeoffs. Friday each one of them would lift the helicopter and maneuver it around a large grassy area. The nurses were encouraged to get a pilot's license but it was not a necessary item. There would always be a pilot aboard, a second pilot who was either a medic or doctor, and the nurse. Three crew on every flight, that is how it worked.

When Wednesday came Rachel was already liking the whole process. She was made for this she felt. This course was extremely advanced, and of course, it would take months with others to become efficient but things were going well. Probably the last 12 years of high intensity work in the ICU and teaching courses in the hospital made her an expert in many facets concerning knowledge and hands on care of the critically ill. It was a science all to itself, not something you learned by reading but rather by doing and seeing the outcomes. Preparing for the unexpected like just when you think someone is stable, they go have a seizure, or cough up blood, their heart sends s a clot to their limb, or maybe it is internal bleeding. Now what?

The helicopter would have blood and plasma available during transport, as well as IV fluids and just about any medication needed. This kind of modern medicine excited Rachel. It was the real deal and she was going to be a part of it. The class thought they should go to dinner Wednesday night and discuss how things were going. Great idea thought Rachel. They should exchange numbers as well. Because they were going to be a part of something quite unique, small, and rare. They chose a Mexican restaurant out by the mall.

Margaritas were ordered by the pitcher, as they were not flying the copters until Friday, and tomorrow was a course review over the material. The four of them bonded in such a short time, each chatting about why they decided to take this route in their careers. They gave up their backgrounds, cities, and hospitals where they learned the skills needed to do this new step in their lives. When the food arrived, they requested a snap shot from the server. Chips n salsa, chimichangas, guacamole, margaritas, and burritos dressed in red peppers and salt made for one happy class. When dessert came, they decided everyone needed a quiz question. Great idea they said. And one by one they quizzed the other with scenarios from a bloody movie!

From gunshot wounds, to highway crashes, pregnant women in labor, a kid pulled from the lake post drowning, and a couple of truckers with legs torn up in a huge accident on the highway. One by one the scenarios played out on the super vigilant nurses in a relaxed setting. Rachel was the first to say that she needed to call it a day and get home to her son and study a little more. On the way home she thought about Seth and the terrible storm they got caught up in. She remembered her head injury which could have been a lot worse. Instead, she just made for a great painting which Seth later painted from the sketch of her. She needed to see how that turned out or if he had finished it yet. In fact, next week she would take the kids over there to his place for a visit. They had not seen him in a long time and they liked him, liked being with him on the sailboat. These next three weeks were all planned out. This week was her five-day course, which she absolutely loved thus far. Next week she would visit Seth with the kids, maybe he would have them over sometime for a sleepover. And the third week she would focus on getting a new job with this course certificate. Her friend at the hospital did not want to see her leave but gave her a tip on a helicopter rescue service at a nearby airport. After she passed the course this week she would apply and maybe secure an interview the following week. Yup, Rachel was a planner.

Thursday came and she was ready. The students would do mock drills of almost every scenario in the book. It was a day to be hands ready, automatic, and do without thinking after many drills. It was tiring and by late afternoon they needed a break. Tomorrow was the big day, take a test, perform active drills, and fly a helicopter for 100 yards off the ground fifty feet high. The last thing left today was to do a mock run with the student in the driver's seat. Rachel opted to go first. All aboard and strapped in she lifted the copter up to fifty feet, hovered, then maneuvered it forward, turned it and steered it to the destination, then lowered it safely to the ground. This was in no way a certificate to fly one just an in-case situation of a disaster. She had to admit it was very exciting!

Friday morning Rachel had a second cup of coffee and brought with her a couple oatmeal raisin cookies, her favorite and she thought she deserved this treat. Today she would pass with flying colors and tomorrow she would email the rescue business for a job. Everyone assembled in the conference room over near St Petersburg near the naval station and air force base. Equipment was everywhere at this high security airport. This is where the final test was to be. Some of the air force pilots were training for positions to be a rescue helicopter pilot. Cool.

Silently and intently the four of them took the written test. It had over 200 questions and required two short essays about two scenarios. Your writing skills needed to be top notch, legible, and accurate. This was no baby's game. Everything must be to the best of the ability of the rescuer. Otherwise, you are out, back on the ground.

After lunch a hands-on test was required for which, they had repeatedly practiced and all scored very high. Finally, the helicopter pilot test, mainly for review. The instructor wanted to see that in a bad, very bad situation; you could get out of there. At the end of this day, this week Rachel said goodbye to her new friends, would be flight nurses, and drove home. Over the skyway bridge she glided on land looking out to the sea and smiling at what she had accomplished. It had taken many years to get here. Be proud Rachel, be proud.

She stopped at a pizza place and sat down to order a to-go pizza. She waited on the beer, or wine, she would have that at home. Once in her place she might even dance or something. She did feel like celebrating. Should she wait until the results came in? Maybe. Two pepperoni pizzas, one with the works and one with mushrooms. The boys would probably eat the whole two pizzas and there would be no leftovers. That would be okay she thought. She needed to cook this week as she had given them frozen dinners all week long. And hot dogs with chips. She dreamed of lasagna and salad with cherry pie and whipped topping.

Rachel snuck three pieces as she knew they would take every piece. She poured a big glass of wine and sat out on the back deck staring at the ocean sipping her wine. She put her feet up on the table and slung back in the chair. She put a song on via her cell phone. How nice it felt.

The boys, Henry, and Patrick, played a familiar game on the tv screen. Xochi was playing with dolls in her room. They were having a sleepover party but getting dressed up to go dancing first. Once they were dressed, she put them in a car and drove them across town (play) and went into the dance place. They drank juice and ate cookies.

Rachel was off in some faraway land when she got a ping. She opened her eyes, took a big sip of wine, and picked up her phone. She opened it and scrolled her texts. It was from the instructor.

Rachel, you passed every segment from today, and, you received the highest score amongst your peers. You are extremely qualified to do this job and do it well. We suggest in your future you take a course and obtain your pilot's license for helicopters and planes. We offer all of that right here and with these high scores your course would be free. Good luck!

3
Seth's Place Downtown

Rachel's high over the weekend after passing her course, swimming in the ocean, cooking a couple meals, and calling her mother simmered into the new week. She phoned Seth and asked if she could come over and bring the kids with her for a visit. He said sure thing. In fact, he said have them bring a suit case and plan to stay over for a couple nights. Their uncle missed them he added. Great said Rachel. She would have a couple nights to herself. She liked the friendship she had with him, and the perks she received. What could she do for him? Nothing he said, unless you wanted to get back into the ongoing mysterious business that Scarlet offered him. Her eyes brightened. Her mind shut down. No. I cannot do that. But if you ever need a weekend off, I could watch monitors or go out scouting for you. As long as they do not look like your beautiful friend Valeria Dave. No, no one is as attractive nor sinister looking as him. That is why he is the perfect double agent he recalled. She totally agreed. He told her to come over and he would order food, then give them a tour of his new place, and the kids could stay two nights. That way if she ever needed a place for them to go, they would be comfortable and she could just drop them off in an emergency. Especially since she was getting into the business of emergencies. She smiled. He did think quite nicely of her.

They loaded into her car, suitcases, and all. Of course, Henry could not miss out on this adventure. A high-rise downtown, say no more. Very cool he spoke to Rachel. He would act the part of the responsible big brother. This he promised. Rachel knew Henry had it in him to be just that but she also knew he liked to go the extra mile when it came to exploring and adventure. Maybe she saw herself in him. Maybe. Just maybe one that is interested and wants to explore gets into more danger, is not as afraid as others. Possibly, this is what leadership is all about. You must take risks, calculated or not, sometimes a risk is worth it. Less times you get a shock or a wakeup call. Balance is moderation. Risk is not knowing everything but knowing you want a good outcome. Search for that path, keep going. Love others and everything works out in the end. She was sounding like some self-help book she had not read. Oh, this was it, she was coming to a crossroads in her life. She had kids, a new career coming, an ending with a former boyfriend, a new house on the beach, and possibly a new life. Things were looking up. Yup.

"Mom, will I get my own room?" Xochi asked.

"Do you want your own room?" Rachel replied.

"Yes, if he has many rooms. Yes."

Xochi was becoming sure of her space. She asked questions. She called Rachel Mom. And now when going to a new place with a familiar person, she asked her for her own room. Rachel saw that as a step in the right direction. Making herself comfortable, making herself a priority meant little Xochi had needs and was letting Rachel know.

The expanding city on the bay had expansion written all over it, yet it had a small city quaintness and scenic look to it. New circles were put in for drivers to turn without lights. Secretly Rachel called these circles of death as she just recently learned how not to get a horn blared at you. Little houses becoming new shops painted in pastel colors and condos going up everywhere. Seth had told her he was near Pineapple and Coconut Ave. Once you are there I am not far. She had Patrick find the address on her phone and direct her the rest of way.

A new selection of palm trees lined the street and she made the turn into the garage to park her car. All departed and grabbed their suitcases, then walked to the exit door. They found the elevators and loaded in. Henry asked her the floor number. We must first go to the lobby as we must be let in to his floor she told them.

"Security." She spoke that to Henry.

"For sure. Yeah man." He raised his eyebrows. This was getting cooler by the minute. Henry had adventures but not in the realm of any money or riches. He was being enlightened. Enriched.

A security desk was on the third floor and a doorman greeted them. A call was placed to Seth on the 12th floor, top floor, and he responded, "Send them up!"

The doorman would escort them and run the elevator for them. The boys' eyes were askance.

Xochi was oblivious to this response. Internally the boys were like thinking how do we navigate with dressed doormen watching us? There must be a key. So, Henry asked, "Is there a key which opens the way up to his floor?"

"But of course, he will give you his key that allows you to descend to the facilities. You place the card over this area, like this, and press your floor. Quite easy." The doorman gave the boys instructions.

"Super, very easy." Patrick noted. Rachel looked at her son as he laid his eyes to the floor.

The hallway off the elevator was magnificent. Art work adorned the walls that drew your eyes in for a look. Were they real paintings? And the carpet was plush, colorful, with swirls and angles. Windows were at each end overlooking the city to the east and the bay to the right. They were only four condos on each floor and they walked to Seth's then rang the doorbell.

Someone answered in a suit. Wow. Did Seth have an attendant inside his place, or maybe he had a cook or servant? All of them studied the man as he gestured his arm and hand to come on in.

"Come in, please come in. Very glad to see my extended family!" The man boasted with glee.

Rachel eyed the man up and down and back down again.

"Good afternoon, Seth. Here is your company." Said the doorman to the gentleman.

"Where's the pirate?" Xochi asked.

After a few double takes, and laughter, they walked in and

shook their heads at the transformation of Seth. The pirate look was gone. Completely shaven, cut hair, no earrings, tailored suit, polished shoes, jewelry on his wrists and a tie set the tone for a very different man, until he spoke.

"Guys, it is me. Seriously, still a pirate underneath, the clothes are for the art gallery I purchased. I must have a business look to do business. No more sail boats and swimming in the ocean. It is cars, biking, and cooling off in the pool."

"Approve?"

"Yes. I approve. You clean up well, even better than your Instagram photo."

"Ok. Let us do a tour, you'll find your room, then we shall have a party."

Seth's condo had four bedrooms, a study, a large living room, a kitchen, a dining room, a balcony, four bathrooms, a washroom, and a bar or sunroom near the balcony. Perfectly decorated in a mix of an ocean color palette and a big city minimalism with tokens of a world charm set in the dining and breakfast areas ever so slightly. Rachel liked it, so did her clan. Seth's room was especially nice as it had a Bahamas feel. Those islands tucked down there not far from Florida where hustle and bustle did not exist. And stories of old times surrounded by pirates, ships, and storms came alive when treasure was discussed.

Seth's bed was a four-poster dark wooden queen size bed with matching furniture. He did have good taste and it showed. She was impressed. Good for him. They were done;

she was sure of it. They would not be best friends, but would remain friendly like an aunt or uncle. When kids were involved, you just could not cut someone out. It was family. Family wins. Nobody was blood related but an important person is just that, important. People form bonds that should be maintained, worked through, and relied upon. Rachel expected if Seth married one of his art students she would be invited to their wedding. Maybe even the kids would have a part of it as well. Marriage. What was she thinking? Must be the condo, it made for a nice home.

"Who is hungry or thirsty?"

All the kids responded yes. Rachel nodded. She responded with a yes to wine. The kids found their play spot and Rachel and Seth sat at his custom bar. He turned some music on, and now, this was their time to talk.

The beautiful dark wooden bar with a lip edge made for a stunning look in this modern upscale condo situated downtown Sarasota. Glass lined shelves adorned each side of a mirror with bottles of alcohol set out across the bottom shelf from end to end. Clean with a ship look in the décor and old-world glassware, Seth poured them a rum and coke with a twist of lime and handed her the barware.

"I will serve you a wine with dinner. Now is your rum drink. Cheers." They clinked glasses, drank, and began the back and forth of friends, former lovers, and now aunts and uncles.

"Life is difficult is it not?" Rachel began.

"However, I know we fell back in love again, but you were

our savior. I could not have done that job heist without you. You saved me. I am forever grateful."

"I suppose it was natural to sleep together on a sailboat under a category one hurricane while searching for fentanyl out at sea. Who would believe that?" Her words sounded crazier than the actual event.

"Even I do not believe that escapade!" Seth realized.

"But madam Scarlet paid us well. Now I have a savings account for a future house."

"She pays perfectly well, because she helps persons along the way. She truly cares and that is why she has millionaires who donate to her cause. God love her." Seth continued.

"Tell me, what is next? You look all set up, Mr. Art Dealer." Rachel could not help but tease this one. He has transformed into yet another character.

"Yes. An art dealer, gallery owner, and teacher of pupils."

"Teacher? You should have been an actor. I would come watch your performances."

"Do not give me any more ideas. I have enough. After this I shall settle down and have kids."

"Kids? Without a mate?"

"Oh, I meant get a wife, have kids, buy a house, or live here."

"I bet you will fall right into that."

"It could have been you." He could not resist. He had to say it. This was their end and it must be discussed.

"Yes. It came close and we experienced a pull out of nowhere but then magically our lives both changed. Seth, you needed to deal with a lighter path in life. The danger was outweighing your future. I am happy Scarlet gave you this new avenue.”

“And you were a mother, a triumphant hero on the water, looking for more adventure while I was winding down. Our paths crossed but did not join. And that is okay.”

“Cheers to that. Well said. Perfectly. To us.”

They sipped drinks at the bar and took in a moment of silence. Some Caribbean music played.

It was during the silence Rachel remembered two more items she needed to talk with Seth about. One was if he would watch the kids when she got a job being a flight nurse and the other was about the painting of her on the sailboat with the injured head.

“Absolutely, anytime. And if I must travel, there is a sitter or two who live in the building with respectable resumes and references.”

“Wonderful.”

Seth got up and told Rachel to wait and stay seated. He went into the living room and looked behind a sofa for something. He turned and lifted it out. The painting was of her.

4

Waterside Interview

Rachel had to get up and take a closer look. The painting was extraordinarily good. How is that so? "It is so good," she exclaimed.

"I take it you like it. It became my solitude, my escape. I poured my soul into this seascape with the beautiful Rachel, bloodied, hurt, but navigating our sails through rough water, then when the eye opened to a calmness it became magnificent." He leaned the painting against the coffee table, then retrieved a second painting, this one had the waves, the storm.

"A second painting?" She encountered two distinct visions. That was Seth's purpose. He was a genius with his knowledge but she did not know how good an artist he was.

"The first one is *The Calm Between Storms,* and the second one is *The Storm.*"

"I really did not know you painted this well. I had seen you draw and thought you might have just found your new direction. I guess you most definitely did."

"Hearing you say they are good makes it real. Thank you."

"I will be saving up some money to buy a couple paintings when your gallery opens."

"Perfect. I will save you some good paintings. A few of

them I may make into prints, which means more people will enjoy them and the cost will come down some."

"Maybe I will paint your kids on the beach this week. Permission?"

"Granted."

A timer went off in the kitchen. "Dinner is ready."

Seth had made a huge lasagna, garlic bread n butter, salad, and a cherry cobbler with vanilla ice cream for dessert. Everyone ate and passed around plates for seconds. Seth insisted the kids were on dish duty, so he could do some computer work and Rachel needed to get home and apply for a special job.

The pair, once very close and intimate, gave each other a hug and a good luck send off. They would keep in touch with updates, gallery openings, new job offers, and kid sleep overs.

*

Rachel went home and went straight to bed. Her day had been enough. Tomorrow she would forge ahead in search of opportunities. For some reason her dreams were livid and she was back again on the sea. The sea that tormented her being that night on the sailboat. She awoke and got up to look out at the ocean. It was calm, no waves. At least it was not a nightmare. And it was over. She smiled and slept in peace the rest of the night. The next morning, she was lit with energy and maneuvered around making coffee, eggs, biscuits with honey, and strawberries and watermelon. She brought her plate to the table, placed her phone next to it and drank her lemonade with fresh squeezed lemon juice and scrolled through her emails. There it was. She read it, got the name of the business, and then went to Google to check it out.

Rocco's Air Rescue near Tampa Bay. She began reading about the business and looked at a couple pictures. Then she went to Maps and put in the address. It looked close by once you went back into town near the highway. From her house out here maybe a 30-45" trip but 15" if you were in Palmetto by the river. The website said he ran hurricane hunter missions May through November and helicopter rescues in every season. There was an email and a phone number. She wrote both down for later use.

Rachel dove heartily into her breakfast and decided she needed to work out today. It had been a while and she needed to maintain her strength and stamina for her new career. First though she sent a resume via the email as instructed via the website. She wrote a small email explaining what she was looking for and that a friend had recommended his service. Then she went to get dressed to go for a run/walk outside. She was at the door when the phone rang. She better answer it because her kids were elsewhere.

She did not recognize the number so she put the phone back down. If they left a message then she would listen and respond when she came back. She exited and began walking north on the sidewalk, beachside, and strolled past the houses and condos. It was a nice morning and this is just what she needed to get her day moving. She ran for a spell and then retreated to walking. She never was a runner and did not plan on becoming one today. She wondered if she could make it all the way to the bridge which crossed over the inlet. She estimated that to be about two miles. Might as well. So off she went with her walking jogging walking routine. She forgot water so she would have to wait until she got home. A couple places she noted had boards on their windows preparing for the hurricane in about ten days. Ten days away was still a long time. There was plenty of time for preparation. She told herself to prepare about five days in advance for food and water and putting away of deck items from the pool. She made it to the bridge and turned around after a brief pause to watch the boats go out to sea and some come back in after maybe an early morning fishing trip. The park was just ahead and by noon the parking lot would be more than half full. It was a busy place, an active tourist site and gathering place for families. Maybe she should plan a picnic for her family sometime. Bring food, toys, chairs, frisbees and surfboards so the kids could have a day and meet up with friends. At her beach house they had a very private beach which was super nice but it might be fun for them to see other kids, plus the place had a café for food and drinks and volleyball on the beach. There was even music. Some other day she said.

She made it back home and headed for the shower. Her shower was extremely fancy, probably the nicest shower she had ever been in. After washing she put a robe on and checked her phone. She had three missed calls from the same number. She dialed it back.

"Hello, Rocco speaking."

"Rocco. I am returning your call. This is Rachel."

"Rachel. So glad you called back. I wanted to touch base with you before I had to go up and do some flying today."

"Here I am. You must have received my email with my resume about employment."

"I sure did. And I am hiring. In fact, I need two persons, two rescue nurses."

"There is only me. But I did meet three others in class."

"Would you like to interview and see if the job is for you?"

"Yes. I would love to do that."

"Can you meet Thursday evening at Watersides? We will conduct it there. Okay?"

"Yes. What time is that?"

"How does seven o'clock sound?" Rocco asked.

"Sounds great. See you there."

"Meet at the bar inside." Rocco instructed.

"Okay." She responded and then hung up. "A dinner interview. That is a first, first of its kind."

She walked to her wardrobe in the closet. What would she wear? Be professional, be casual, be sporty and capable? Be honest and forthright, maybe he really needed people, so hiring might go very well. Easy peasy she thought. Not so fast said her mind. He was the pilot and owner which meant he knew everything and ran it by himself. Be on your toes, maybe do a shot of tequila before hand and then she laughed. Be yourself.

In the end Rachel opted for sexy casual, after all he picked a coastal restaurant at seven pm, which made that a date. She had not been on a date in quite a long time. She wore rust-colored long pants, a loose off white cotton shirt with jewelry on her wrists and neck, accompanied by a leather purse and sandals. Perfect. She tied her back with a clip that resembled a pearl. She had makeup on with lipstick and her nails had been recently polished with color. She was thirty-five and looked pretty good, One would think she was on a date or meeting someone to flirt with. Ha ha. This was an interview by the boss. She arrived early and sat at the bar, ordering an ice water.

Rocco cleaned up for tonight's interview. He had not hired in a while and really needed a couple new employees to keep things running. He totally enjoyed what he did and did not seem to lack for anything. He thought why not have dinner at the same time? When he walked into the Waterside restaurant and headed for the bar, he did not expect to see such an amazing looking woman seated all by herself. It could not be her he thought. He had not seen anyone else look as stunning as Rachel did when he first laid eyes upon her. He smiled. How sweet.

She turned around and looked his way. She saw a beautiful man with dark hair, dark eyes, and a brownish beard coming her way. Was this Rocco? No way. How adorable. She smiled. Oh my gosh, be professional. Stand up sweetie and greet him. He put out his hand and asked, "Rachel?"

"It is Rachel. Rocco?"

"Rocco, yes. Pleased to meet you." He smiled again. They looked at one another somewhat struck in surprise.

"Would you like to sit at the bar or a table?"

"Whatever you prefer." She stated elegantly.

"Let us order a drink and sit at this lovely bar, then retreat to a table after a few questions."

"Sounds good."

The bartender approached them and alerted them to the daily specials for drinks and tonight's dinner items, offered them menus, and gave them a moment. They decided do drink margaritas. Really, on an interview? Oh my, another first. Secretly, Rachel said to herself might as well call this a date. How fun. He might be a good fun guy to work for. Get ready to be questioned and then her questions in return. When the margaritas came, they clinked glasses to helicopter nurse rescue careers. Then he pulled out his paper form and asked her questions and checked the boxes off on the list. After one page of questions, he was finished. Did she have any questions for him he asked? The bartender brought them a second drink, a spicy margarita, with a red pepper and red rimmed salted glass. "Your turn," he said.

"What kind of nurse are you looking for?"

He looked at her, looked away, and back at her. "Someone just like you."

"Then let me tell you I have two kids, I am single, so I do the best I can. I do have a back up plan with help to watch them but no other family around."

"Perfect. We both have kids to watch and care for, and I

have a grandmother who lives with me, so I have back up right in the house."

They smiled and then she asked a couple more questions.

"What are you doing tomorrow?"

"Tomorrow?"

"Yes, tomorrow."

"My kids come back tomorrow morning."

"Perfect. Bring everyone over to the hangar at the airport and I will give them all a tour."

"Okay. I know they will love that."

"You hungry? Let us get a table, order and eat."

At dinner they talked about this and that. There were no more work questions. They found a hundred different topics to discuss. They were enjoying themselves so much they forgot about the interview.

5

The Hangar

The next day Rachel went and picked up the kids from Seth's and proceeded to hear all about their last three days from swimming in the ocean, the pool, driving around in his fancy orange car, and cooking for him one night, playing his video games, and staying up late and sleeping in. You would have thought they spent a week at grandma's house with no rules.

"Was there candy or ice cream?"

"Yes, lots of it!" Xochi exclaimed.

"I have a surprise for you guys today. I think you will like it."

"What is it? Tell us. Are we going there now?"

"We are, but first let us get a drive through lunch."

Rachel found a drive through that pleased everyone. Good. It would be quiet while she drove them to the hangar. She made her way over the bridge to a sleepy little town on the north side of the river and then up some two-lane road to another quiet little unincorporated town near the south end of Tampa Bay. There was a chain link fence out by the road. She turned in and heard the kids ask, "An airport? Why are we going to an airport? Are we flying today?"

"My surprise is a tour of an airport hangar, where they keep the planes and hang out, I suppose."

"Cool. Is this someone you know?" asked Patrick.

"The owner of the airport and hangar is the business I applied to work for once I get my certificate for the flight nurse rescue course I took last week."

They were busy looking out the windows to ask any more questions.

"If you will please be courteous and do not touch everything. Be considerate. This could be my boss if he hires me."

"We will be on our best behavior, just for you, mother." Patrick took the lead.

"Yes, yes, we will make sure he hires you." Henry speculated.

"Of course, he will hire you, you are so pretty and smart." Xochi was sweet and loving.

"Why would a pilot hire a nurse?" asked Henry.

Patrick explained to him about his mom taking a course to work on a helicopter and rescue injured people from all over. "Henry, when they have to get to the hospital fast, or go to a specialty place for a certain kind of treatment."

"Life flight I think they call it. You must be very important Miss Rachel, an expert I would say."

"Yes, Henry, an expert in my area but working as a team."

"Here we are." She parked over by the small house not too far from the runway as instructed via Rocco. He came out to greet them and brought little Johnny with him. An older woman followed behind them.

Violet came right over to Rachel and her brood and

introduced herself. "Hello, you must be Rachel. I am Violet, Rocco's grandmother, and great grandma to this guy Johnny."

Rachel nodded and said, "I am Rachel and this is Patrick, my son, and his friend, Henry, and this little one is Xochiquetzal, my beautiful little daughter."

Xochi and Johnny smiled at each other. She would have a playmate.

Rocco greeted Rachel, "Hello Rachel, ready for a tour of your new place to work?"

Her eyes met his. "Really, you are hiring me?"

"Yes, you have the job. We can talk specifics tomorrow."

"Tomorrow?"

"I thought if you are not busy, we could take the big old plane up and out tomorrow, the one I use for hurricane measurements."

"Violet makes a big brunch on Saturday mornings, enough to feed an army. Everyone is welcome to come back, eat and play while I take up my newest employee for a spin."

"Okay, that works. And I do not have to make breakfast or lunch is more perfect. Can I bring anything to help Violet?"

"I suppose if you are going to the store pick up a couple of muffin and cookie boxes and I will have the kids cook while you are flying. I should have everything else as I went to the store yesterday. I will be making most of it tonight."

"Violet loves to cook in a big way. Eat very light like fruit or just coffee before we fly. That way your stomach will have nothing to settle in case of turbulence."

"Well, Rocco, I do not get air sick." Rachel told him.

"But have you ever been on a cargo plane, the big guy, with all the noises and bouncing it does?"

"No, I have not."

"Then eat light, very light."

She nodded in agreement.

"Let us head to the hangar and I will show you where we hang out during storms or severe weather, or before and after work trips. It is like a mini apartment, or rather large open apartment."

Johnny and Xochi ran to the front to lead the way. All followed. Violet retreated to the house to bring out a snack.

Johnny opened the back door to the hangar and everyone made their way in. It was expansive with three walls, the back and two sides and a large rolling front door which was up now. There was no plane in the hangar, just couches, tables, a workshop, and a small kitchen area with a refrigerator, stove top, microwave, and eating area. In the back left corner, there was a bathroom with shower, and over in the back right corner there was a small work area with shelves for storage. The left front area was the eating and kitchen area and the front right area held supplies and tools. In the middle there was room for an airplane, but no plane.

Out the front one could see airport runways and beyond that more grass and the ocean or bay after that. It was quite pretty thought Rachel. Rocco pulled out some footballs, bikes, and other games and put them out front. He had arranged a few chairs to sit outside. He offered Rachel and the kids a drink. Violet came in with a tray of snacks and set it one the table. She joined Rocco and Rachel for a chat out front. He instructed them to stay close by, no exploring today. Another day he would take them on a grand tour, and if mom said yes, eventually on a plane ride.

The walls were decorated with pictures mostly of Rocco, his parents, and numerous airplanes. Helicopters, too. Rachel looked around, there was so much to take in. She did notice some landscapes pictures but could not place them in the US.

"Where are these picturesque places?" She pointed to a block of enlarged photos.

"Those are my father's hometown in Ireland and these are my mother's hometown in South America, Brazil, to be exact."

"Lovely. Very pretty."

"Yes, many memories up on the walls. Many more memories to make as well." He added.

"Life gives us much to be appreciative of, for sure." She looked upon her brand-new family of two kids she did not have a year ago.

Rocco looked at Rachel when she said this. She seemed like a very nice person and he liked to listen to her speak. He decided right then and there he was going to ask her out next Friday night to go out on the town. He would ask her after the air tour tomorrow.

They sat and watched the kids play and learned about each other and Violet. Quite a pleasant day and she had a job. She toasted to her adult company and thanked Rocco again. He said they would talk about the details tomorrow.

After a couple hours passed by Rocco remembered he had

something important to show to his new friends, the kids. "Hey guys, come see something that I recently made. It is specific for hurricanes, those slow-moving monster storms that can wipe out and destroy everything along the way."

He led them to the back right of the hangar where he pulled off the shelf a very large bowl.

"I have been working on these bracelets for hurricanes. You wear it and the light it emits can be seen up in the sky to a plane in search of finding those stranded or hurt. You put it on and hold up the arm and the wrist to the sky. The warmth of your wrist and the darkness of the sky make it be seen. I need testers."

"Sign me up." Henry said.

"Me too," said Patrick.

"Can I wear one too?" asked Xochi.

"Yes. And here is one for Miss Rachel." Rocco put the bracelet on her and explained how it works.

"You are an inventor?"

"I tinker with concepts from nature hoping they work in rea life. We shall see. Of course, I hope no one is stranded or hurt during a hurricane."

"Maybe if you fly over us, we can flag you and you will see us." Patrick was thinking about the idea, then again, we probably will not be out during a hurricane."

"Most certainly none of us will be out. But if we ever were then we shall hold it up and pray you are flying overhead." Rachel glided through that scenario.

"I think it is time to go. Thanks for the tour and snacks. We shall return tomorrow for brunch. Sounds like a great plan and I will not have much before the flight. Eat after the flight."

Friday night came and Rachel reflected on the past two weeks. She had taken a course for her future and passed with glowing remarks, applied for a job via an email and website, had a dinner interview, then went for a hangar and airport tour, followed by a job offer, and the brunch invitation with an airplane ride in a cargo plane tomorrow. Her head was swirling, her life was spinning in control, and she felt happy. Everything was going so well she was sure there must be even more. She remembered things come in threes. She took a course and passed, she interviewed and received a job offer, and there was a hurricane coming. She told herself, no it can not be the hurricane, there must be one more good thing. Three good things, that is it. She would not hear of the third thing being a hurricane. No way. That sounded like tragedy, a mess waiting to happen. She could not deal with the thought of a hurricane coming now. Just then her phone rang. She recognized the number.

"Hi."

"Hi."

Yes?"

"I know you are coming here tomorrow for brunch and a plane ride. I just wanted to tell you I had a great day. I truly did."

"I did too. Thank you so much for calling and letting me know. I will see you tomorrow."

"Yes. Tomorrow. But I wanted to ask you one more thing

so you could think about it and maybe give me an answer then."

"Okay. Ask away." Rachel allowed.

"Next Friday … I was wondering if you would go on a date with me?"

"A date?"

"Yes, a date. I had the best time on the interview date and today with the kids, I want to ask you out for next Friday. I am asking early because I do not want anyone else to beat me to the ask."

"I am hardly in demand. Let me think a moment."

Rachel paused; she did not want to seem too eager. It was all coming so fast.

A long moment of silence was held between them. No one was thinking. They were just mesmerized by the attraction. It was obvious and apparent.

"I would love to."

Chapter Six

6

The Brunch

Rachel decided last minute she would ask the neighbors daughter home from college to come with them today to watch the kids while she and Rocco went up in his plane. She did not want Violet to cook, serve brunch, then watch four kids for hours. The college student said yes, she would come to the airport and hang out with them.

"Perfect, I am leaving at 10:30. See you then."

They arrived at 11:10 and headed into the small house near the south end of the airport. Rocco greeted them and led them inside. Violet had the table set with plates, silverware, glassware, and a mixed floral setting in the center, mostly fragrant peonies in full bloom. The dining room had a large table with eight chairs and was set in the middle of the house. The kitchen was out back with a picture window facing the airport. The cook had a beautiful view of the bay beyond the runways. The dining room window overlooked a small bed of colorful flowers and a couple of bird baths. Rocco tuned on instrumental mellow music and set the speaker onto the buffet. Violet had placed extra dishes and a mix of drinks on the side board for her company. The tablecloth was white linen and the plates were a floral mix while the napkins were a soft peach color. It was all very pretty to look at.

"The table looks too pretty Violet to get messy."

"I know, but messy we will be. Let us eat while it is hot!"

Each place held a card with a name on it. The kids found their spots and found their manners as well. This was fancy and unexpected. Violet asked them their drink choice and Rocco helped her serve the refreshments. They looked like a team at hand.

"Violet learned all her skills at a very fancy restaurant where she worked. She likes to reproduce the finer things in life." Rocco explained.

"I am impressed and I love it!" Rachel approved and nodded graciously.

The selections were Irish breakfast casserole with corned beef, runny eggs, hashbrown potatoes, white cheddar cheeses, and a little green onion on top. Scones in several flavors such as blueberry lemon iced and strawberry raspberry mix with powdered sugar atop, a Swiss onion pie, a chocolate truffle dessert, in addition to fruit crepes, and a soup with seafood, tomatoes, spinach, and cilantro. And she had made some waffles for the kids with chicken tenders. That with all the goodies made for her crowd and a kid pleaser as well.

"Pass the maple syrup, please," asked Henry.

Both Rachel and Rocco passed on the champagne, they would save it for after the flight.

"Rachel, are you nervous about flying today?" asked Violet. The sitter looked to Rachel for her answer.

"Are you mother?" asked Patrick. Xochi looked to Rachel

for her answer. Rocco looked at her as well.

The table went quiet as Rachel finished a bite of food and put her fork down. "Why no, I am not nervous, should I be?" She deflected back to Rocco.

"Heck no, the big bomber will keep us up in the air floating around the coast. It is a perfect joy ride."

"Joy ride?" Henry repeated.

"It is not like any other airplane. I call it Rough n Ready because I must take her up whether she is ready or not and in the roughest of weather."

"Henry, he is kidding about the joy ride. When you go to the amusement parks and ride the coasters and such, there is a thrill, right?"

"Ah, yes."

"Rough and Ready is a thrill to experience, especially in tumultuous weather. So, I have been told." Violet spoke her truth. "I have never been up in her and do not plan on it."

"You all are scaring my copilot. No more." He stammered out, then laughed.

"Copilot?" Rachel laughed as well. Inside she was thinking *should I be scared or worried?*

"To my new employee I am sure you have been in some bad weather flying. You will be fine. We both will be just fine and we will come back and drink some champagne later and watch the sunset tonight from the upper balcony."

"Watch the sunset? Who is up for watching the sunset tonight?" asked Rachel.

"Please. Pretty please!" Xochi whined.

"Then its set we will have leftovers tonight and watch the sunset. I will make some corned beef sandwiches. Because you will be hungry by nightfall." Violet smiled. She loved her Saturdays, made her feel like the old days. And today the table was full of company. Life was complete for now.

"See you guys at sunset," Rachel finished eating and looked to Rocco for further words.

"The kids will help Violet cleanup."

The sitter said, "Violet you go relax and the kids and I will clean up. I am sure I can find everything to put away the leftovers and do the dishes."

"Sounds nice. Now you two go have a joy ride."

Rocco and Rachel cleared their dishes and left the house. They walked to the hangar and gathered a couple items. Then Rocco led the way to the other hangar where the plane was kept.

He handed her the two water bottles. He opened the hangar door and slid it all the way up to reveal the big Rough and Ready. It was big and a little old she thought. But what did she know?

"I need to do a check, then we can depart." Rocco pointed to a sofa where she could wait. She went and sat and then watched him do a review and walk around the plane. Rocco had dark brown hair and was tall, he also had a mustache and beard, well-trimmed. He appeared fit and his arms were toned. Today he had pants on that were army fatigue in color, worn with a belt and a tight black short sleeved shirt. When he put his sunglasses on, he looked well, say it Rachel as she thought it. "Hot, very hot."

He looked over at her. She shook her head. She did not say a word but she kept looking. He occasionally glanced over at her as well. What was he thinking? Best not look too much, save that for later he thought. Sunset will be here before you know it. Now for the thrill ride in the sky.

This was routine for him. He had been doing this line of work for over seven years. He was good at it. He guessed he liked to make fun of it due to the nature or seriousness business that it was. By making or poking fun it decreased the stress of it all. Not many persons have maneuvered a plane through the eye of a hurricane. Not many at all.

"Let us go! All aboard the Rough and Ready."

Rocco helped Rachel onto the plane as he explained the details from her question "What kind of plane is this?"

"This is a Lockheed-Martin WC-130J aircraft. This plane is on loan to me, I do not own it, but have special privileges for its use. The rest of the 403rd wing is based at Keesler Air Force Base in Biloxi, Mississippi. They wanted to test out this site over here."

"Do you own a plane?"

"Yes, I do. It is for pleasure but I have the helicopter for business. That is where you come in."

"And this is for the hurricanes and the measurements for the weather services."

"Okay. I am ready. I think"

"This is a good practice run for the oncoming hurricane next week or about ten days away."

"Wear these headphones and I will talk to you then." He instructed her.

She gave the thumbs up sign. Rocco turned the ignition on, looked at all the panels and began moving out of the hangar towards the runway. She watched in awe as he moved the plane to the runway. Noises and air swirling and so many buttons. She tried to take it all in. And the whole back was practically open to them. She wondered what the joy ride really meant?

It was then that everything really revved up, that noise that the engine makes before a plane starts down the runway for takeoff. Up and up the noise got louder and louder, she could hear it even through her headphones. "Ready Rachel?"

What? Of course, you think I am going to bow out now. No way. "Yes, I am ready," she said in her little microphone and then she gave a thumbs up for more reassurance of self.

There they were pilot and copilot incognito taking off down the runway. Fast and faster picking up speed, headed right towards the bay. She could see it off in the near distance. Up they went and some of the noise dissipated and Rocco said, "we are up and off we go," with a smile to her big eyes. Out and over the lower south end of Tampa Bay they flew and took a left turn towards the ocean and outer islands. He checked his radar, not much out here today but a couple commercial jets from the two local airports. He flew them past all the land and out to sea.

Rachel looked all around, there was nothing but the big beautiful ocean, right, left and center. Amazing. Rocco pointed to the oil rigs way out front. Oh yeah, she knew those by sea from a few months ago. She had not told him about her secret job with Seth. She probably should. Maybe on her date next Friday. One got a bird's eye view way out here. They appeared smaller, less ominous than those loud creaky steel movements after rust sets in. She saw two but not the third one which was more north. They stayed steady and headed out even further. One could get lost at sea. Maybe that is what he wanted her to see. How could anyone be found way out here?

"How can you find anyone way out here?" She finally asked.

"Very difficult. But with radar, radio, and good eyesight you would be amazed. That and a vigilance for measuring the latitude and longitudinal lines."

"I should brush up on those map skills."

"Mapping the waters is the key Rachel."

She repeated his words. "Mapping the waters is the key."

"Think about all the sharks down there, some have tags and they map them with a shark finder app. They have even named them."

"Yes. I have heard of that."

"So, you think you are going to like this business of flying and saving lives?"

"I already do. Coordinating the two will be the challenge, right? Like timing and getting them to where they need to go."

"You will forget that you are in the air. The pilots do that job while you attend and focus on the heartbeat and stamina of the patient. I think you are going to love it. I know I do.”

“Cool.”

“A couple of times we have life flighted persons off the cruise ships.”

“Seriously?”

“They have a mini hospital on board but could not stay as they needed more care like surgery from a large hospital. Fairly dramatic I must say, one minute cruising the Gulf of America and the next flying through the air over sea on to land and away from the party.”

“Oh my. That is a vacation downer.”

Rocco listened to the radio and tuned in. An afternoon thunderstorm had developed that they would fly through on the return. “Looks like some stormy weather on the way back.”

“Typical.”

“We will try to avoid it but it looks like its near the airport. Ready to return?”

“Yes, sir.”

Rocoo turned the plane to head back in. Now he could see the darkened clouds hovering over the route home. Rachel was going to experience an afternoon thunderstorm in the air. Will be good experience he thought. Though it can be loud and bumpy.

7

Rough and Ready Tour

Rocco looked over to make sure Rachel had her seat belt fastened to prepare for the rocking and a rolling some turbulence that could shake his plane. This was not going to be hurricane winds but he wanted Rachel to enjoy the experience and maybe he wanted her to be assured by his navigational skills. In about ten minutes they would hit the afternoon storm and experience the thrill or joy ride as Violet liked to call it.

"Should I close my eyes as we head back?" She asked him through the microphone.

"If you like but when it begins to be a bit rough keep them open."

"Okay. I will." Rachel closed her eyes and listened to the hum.

A few minutes later the rain came, the clouds were low and obliviating the view at times. If Rachel opened her eyes, she would see that she could not see out the front nor sides.

Rocco decided to drop altitude some but he must have over done it because the drop caused Rachel to open her eyes and feel the swoop.

"I am sorry. Did you feel your stomach drop?"

"Yes. Are we good?"

"Yes. We are. Probably keep your eyes open for a while."

She did as she was instructed. She looked out the front and saw whips of white passing by and really could not see the ground or anything in front of her. They were in the thunderstorm.

There was not anything she could do. She sat there and watched Rocco fly the big cargo plane. The plane started to bounce and lift and drop and even tilt to one side or the other.

She held on to her seat and braced herself. The hits kept coming and coming. She was glad he was flying the plane; her head was swirling some. This must be the thrill ride. A couple of the hits threw her side to side and the whole plane seemed louder and it was dark outside now, almost pitch black out.

Rocco did one more dip in altitude as he needed to see how far away his runway was. He reached his hand over to touch hers as to comfort her. He patted her hand and then focused and dipped lower causing a drop in one's stomach.

"Whoa. Okay I will be fine."

"I warned you about eating before the plane ride. You said you could handle it."

"My stomach is fine actually. It is the movement making me a little dizzy." Rachel expressed.

"Yes, that takes some getting use to. But like a sailor or boater you will get better with time."

"If you say so. Yes, like sea legs, one gets air legs, or wait one gets airhead." She laughed.

One big final dip and now he could see. The clouds were gone but rain hit the windshield. Quickly, though, it lightened and then went away. They were through the storm. Rachel looked out and she could see Tampa Bay. She was sure he could see his airport by now.

"Almost home."

Rocco pointed to the strip. He turned and went south for a few, then did a 180 and lowered more to meet the strip. Soon they would be on land and Rough and Ready would be parked in her hangar garage and be ready for action in another week.

Rachel could see the airport and landing strip. It was topsy turvy, more so than a jet airliner, yet she managed to stay seated, remain calm and not be nauseous. Maybe she passed the first flight test because she had never experienced anything like this. She smiled. Okay let us hit the ground with a soft landing.

Rocco placed the plane perfectly and the landing was sweet without an issue. He got her back in the hangar just in time. The rain came pouring down and the wind picked up. She guessed they just beat the storm. The two of them sat out in the hangar and waited for the storm to pass.

*

Rocco cleaned up the plane some and Rachel rested her eyes. She got a taste of flying in a storm. She knew it would get better, yes better with time. She drifted off for a short nap.

"Ready?"

"Ready for what?"

"Ready for champagne and a rooftop view of the Bay?"

"Yes. Let us go."

*

The kids had had a wonderful time with little Johnny, the college sitter, and Violet. The sunset was about two hours away. Violet pulled out the sandwiches and some leftovers. Time for round number two. Except tonight they would eat outside up on the upper deck which faced the Bay and runway. It was a pretty view and all the rain was gone. The food was brought upstairs and champagne was poured for the adults. You could say it was an after party for the big event.

*

On the ride home everyone shared their day with the car. Henry and Patrick listened attentively to Rachel's discussion of the cargo airplane ride and into the storm. They said a few times they were glad she made it and held her cookies as they say. Rachel reminded the kids that the hurricane was about ten days off, so no chores tomorrow but next week the preparations would be dealt with. She would make a list for the kids to accomplish.

What an interesting week. She felt like her life was advancing in ways she never saw coming. Without warning the future was coming to her. Her life was unfolding and so was hurricane Rebekah. The storm was ten days away.

But Friday, Friday was her date night. Rocco was picking her up and they were going out to dinner and dancing, but first a stop at a champagne bar downtown which just opened. Rachel wore a dress tonight with a semi plunging neckline and flowy skirt below a thick belt. What was she doing? This was her boss. Oh well, stranger things have happened.

The pair sat outside then realized it was too hot and went inside for a cooler temperature. The vibe was fancy and pink. They sipped champagne and shared an appetizer while music played in the background. "Did you recover quickly after the plane ride?"

"Yes, I did fine. Thanks for asking. I wanted to tell you about those oil rigs out there."

"The ones off the coast, the abandoned rigs?"

"Yes. I sailed out there with a coworker and we went fishing and exploring."

"Really?"

"Yes. For several weeks a few months ago."

"Recent then. There was a recent hurricane that deflated out when it hit land."

"We were in it."

"No way. You are lucky to have been fortunate. Were you on the rig at the time?"

"No. I was sailing the boat the whole time. It was very rough that I fell and gnashed my head and it bled everywhere. We had to bandage me up and then I navigated the boat at night while he slept.”

“Brave. No other words for it. Our Rachel is smart and brave.”

“Mr. Rocco, you are the brave one. Fearless for sure.”

“Thank you. But it comes naturally. Guess I was born that way as the singer sings her song.”

“This is delicious champagne, sparkly with a hint of rose.”

“Champagne does make a night special. Indeed.” The couple raised their glasses and toasted to the night.

Tonight, Rocco pulled his hair back as it was about chin length or longer and he looked like a different person Rachel thought. She liked it. He wore chains around his neck and rings on his fingers. He wore an off-white linen loose shirt and jeans. He was casual and dressed down. But he looked relaxed and she liked that.

“This friend of yours, is it a serious friendship or relationship? Three weeks is a long time to spend on a boat together.”

“You are right about the time length but it was work. All I can say is that it was a covert operation for intelligence.” Rachel spit out the goods.

“Rachel, you’re an operative for the US government?”

“No. Not exactly.”

She paused to gather her thoughts. Tell him enough to be honest and nothing more.

“I assisted an operative for a top-secret mission. And we were successful. But I do not work for the Feds, in any capacity.”

"My, my, you are important. Someday, you will tell me. I just know it. I see that you already want to tell me. But you can do that in the future. We have some dinner and dancing to do. The fun stuff!"

As they were about to leave there was a small tv in the bar area and one could see a flashing news report come across the television. Then there appeared to be a helicopter and airplane collision over a river. The news headline said 15 are missing or presumed dead.

The pair looked at one another and walked out and on their way into the night.

*

Rocco had reservations at an elegant restaurant over on one of the nearby islands. They had the best martinis, he hoped she liked a martini. Did not everyone these days? It held a beautiful fish tank in the center and the place was quiet. It was not season in Florida right now, that came after hurricane season and near the holidays. This was their first real date out together. For him it seemed magical and her the same. They chatted about many topics but settled on the collision they viewed from the news. Because his business was helicopters and planes, and hers was rescue. But when the two collided there might not be any rescue. No one to rescue the injured because maybe no one made it through the fiery crash.

He asked her a bold question about her heart. "Have you

been in love before?"

She raised her eyebrows to think. "Maybe, because I thought I was, it was love. But honestly, likely no. I was in excitement."

"Excitement."

"And have you been in love?"

"With airplanes. And my little brother, but not in love with a woman. No."

"Such honesty is refreshing. I know I do love my new family, the kids. They light up my life."

"That is refreshing and giving, caring for little ones."

"Rocco, do you want children?"

"Sure, a blessing they will be for both of us."

"Sweet." She noticed he said us, that made it personal.

The meal arrived and the pair devoured the steaks with sides and drank their martinis.

*

The calmness of the night belied their working lives and the stress they naturally took on almost every day. For the third venue Rocco took her to a piano bar to listen to live music and singing. The evening had cooled down and a slight breeze lifted their hair now and then. Inside they enjoyed the music and danced a couple slow tunes. Rachel thought the night perfect. What a lovely date. What a lovely night out downtown. He drove her home and walked her to the door. Then gave her a first kiss. Which lingered. And, she asked him to come in and watch the ocean out back. He replied he would love to. And they walked through the door into Rachel's house on the beach.

She guided him to the kitchen and poured a glass of wine for both. She gave him a mini tour and then they went out back to sit on her deck and listen to the sound of waves.

"Do you need music?"

"I do not. Play some if you like."

She clinked her glass to his. "Maybe later."

Rachel did not play her playlist or any idea what she was doing tonight. She let it flow and realized she had not stopped smiling. Easy peasy.

8

The Beach House Bedroom

Rachel remembered her sister's words one time when she questioned her about sex. She responded, "Everyone loves sex, sister." Sure, thought Rachel. But isn't it a more profound experience when it is special? She supposed one could have sex like sport, to do it and get it over with, kind of like a job. But for Rachel, no, she wanted more. She wanted the intensity, the pleasure, the moment to last not just a moment but for hours, and then into weeks, and months.

"Penny for those silent thoughts?"

"No, Rocco, you would need much, much more than a penny."

Rachel turned the music on and hit play. She and Rocco sipped more wine and talked about themselves, the conversation that one has when they first meet and want more. She felt like she knew him for a long time. Everything was easy, polite, and he seemed to be concerned for her wellbeing. Like maybe he was looking out for her. She liked that. She also cared for him, and it was growing by the day. She had known him almost two weeks now. She turned to stare at him bringing her thoughts in sync with her vision. What did she see?

She saw a handsome man, sexy, with dark hair and brown

eyes, and a mustache and beard. She had never kissed a man with all that facial hair. Might be exciting, like it was on her front porch. She would like to do that again. He had responsibilities like she did. They had a similarity with family obligations. They shared a commonality; what else did they share?

"Should we split that dessert?" she asked him.

"I am ready. Sounds good." He lifted his glass to finish the wine and picked up the speaker and followed behind Rachel to the kitchen.

She grabbed two forks from the drawer and placed the chocolate cheesecake dessert on the marbled counter. The kids were staying overnight at Henry's house down the road. This crossed Rachel's mind and she relaxed even more. Rocco looked for a lighter as he saw Rachel had a couple candles on the counter. She pointed to the drawer next to the stove top.

"Oh, this is delicious. I will never not like chocolate," said Rachel.

"I happen to love it as well. We should experiment though, maybe we are missing out."

She fed him a bite when he was lighting her candles. She licked her own lips and then lifted some whip cream from the delicacy and enjoyed this indulgent. The candles flickered the music played and two souls became mesmerized by the closeness igniting electricity and a pull they could not contain. She poured them each a glass of water that they sipped.

Rocco looked at his date and saw a beautiful woman who had responsibilities and worked so hard caring for others, using her knowledge and skills to become a skilled flight nurse to save more lives. They were one and the same and he was realizing that at this moment. He wanted to be with her. He wanted to kiss her more, to find out how soft and passionate she was. The look in her eyes told him she wanted him too. He would take this slow to make sure. He wanted no hesitancy, only confirmation and truth. He walked towards her and touched her arm moving his hand up to her shoulder and over to her face where he caressed her cheek and put her hair behind her ear and then kissed it.

Rachel leaned some and allowed his passion to touch her and kiss her down her neck. His lips felt so nice, and she longed for a man, this kind and secure man. Then he took hold of her face with both hands and brought her face to his and kissed her lips, open and parted and with intense passion and strength he pushed his tongue inside and kissed his Rachel. She returned the fervor with her gentle ways and longing. She was relenting to this man in her kitchen. And she liked it.

He did too. His eyes bore into hers and asked her in silence do you want me?

She picked up a candle and said, "You bring the other one."

Quietly, he followed her into the bedroom where she placed a candle on the dresser and he placed one on a nightstand. They did not need music but he went back to retrieve the speaker and turned it down low, then placed it on the other nightstand. The romantic dance continued for some time slowly and then quickened with a pace of urgency. She kissed her guy again and again. He caressed her skin her softness exciting him and filling him with desire. He never wanted this to stop. He might have to make love to her all night long and then again tomorrow maybe. He kissed her back and held her head for steadiness. He laid on top of this gorgeous woman and inside declared himself the happiest man on earth. Rachel, he thought to himself you have no idea how happy I am to have found you and to be with you.

This romantic dalliance continued throughout the night and quieted before the dawn of day. The candles had burnt out and Rocco had stopped the music so they rested their bodies across the bed and fell into slumber with smiles spread across the two faces.

Rachel rose and found two robes for them to dress in and make some breakfast. "Here you go, you are staying for breakfast, right?"

"Absolutely, if you allow me to make it."

"I sure will. I will just grab things and set them on the counter for you to cook and I will set the table for two. My kids do not come back until dinner time."

"That works out for me as I do not have any work, or missions today. I am all yours if you want me." He stated.

"Yes. We did not discuss that on our date last night. Thank you for a wonderful evening."

"And thank you for coming out with me. And extending the evening here was enchanting." Rocco meant every word. They just clicked he thought.

She smiled at him while he cooked breakfast. She thought they just hit it off naturally. Cool thought Rachel.

"Tell me more about your family from Ireland and South America," Rachel asked as she ate her cheese omelet.

"What would you like to know?"

"All of it. It sounds extraordinarily unique."

Rocco sat down and started eating and then paused to tell his story of how he came to America. His dad fled Northern Ireland during the bombing era and went to South America. He met his mother in Brazil. They dated and later wed and lived there for a while. Their desire though was to move to America and so they did. Rocco was born six months later after arrival in America. He was schooled in the US learning English. Later when grown he joined the Air Force and when finished with that he joined his parents in Florida and bought this old airport, ran a helicopter business, and began the hurricane hunter missions when the government loaned him this old Rough and Ready. His parents became pregnant with another child by surprise and had little Johnny five years ago. Tragically, they both died in a car accident. So, grandma Violet and himself care for the young one. Talk about a blended family with a variety of ages. But it all works. "And here I am having met the most wonderful and beautiful lady I believe I have ever seen."

"You are too kind. You flatter me and I love it."

"It is true, everything I say is true. You will become a great flight nurse over the next year I am sure of it. We may have to hire another nurse as well. More people have moved down here so more accidents are occurring."

She looked at him and reflected on his history. He has had

a productive life and she was sorry about losing his parents.

"How about your family besides the two I have met and their best friend?"

"My life. I am a cardiac nurse, worked recently at a Mexican restaurant for fun, inherited two children this past year. I love being a mom. I have not married or felt to in my life. My career is just where I want it to be. I joined up with an old friend from high school to do the sailing venture a few months ago. I did it to save lives from cartel fentanyl reaching the streets and killing the children. We pulled off a successful sting. I am out of that business for good. I think."

"And your parents are they still alive and well?"

"Yes, both are alive and well in Ohio. Retired and doing this and that. We love to eat perch sandwiches when we visit up on Lake Erie. You might like it. They have a small airport near town."

She paused.

"My mom has Irish roots and my dad has English."

"Tell me more."

"You want the nitty gritty, whole shebang, Okay. Ready?"

"I am listening."

"My grandmother was one of eight children. Her father worked on a vineyard. He was from Germany. Her name was Pearl and she worked at a crayon factory up by the lake. She had my mother out of wedlock in a period of time one did not do that sort of thing. Women she knew would go to the next state over and have abortions and never tell anyone. She decided to keep her baby and raise it all by herself. Later in life she said her daughter was the best thing that ever happened to her. 'Put that in your pipe and smoke it' is a saying my mother use to say about something absurd. My grandfather turned out to be a farmer, a good one, who had lots of land, But Pearl never told him about the baby. So, he never knew her. How sad. I saw a picture of him at the Knights of Columbus Club in town, he must have been a knight or something. It said he bought a playground for the children and had the equipment set up. He did that. It almost tells me he knew about her. My aunt, grandma's sister Cora told me to go and tell him the story, that he would want to know. I did just that. It was meddling but by this point the old folks would die and the poor guy deserved to know. I walked to his house, like five miles, along the railroad tracks. Probably could have gotten myself killed. The things you do when you are young can be rebellious in nature, ya know. You do not think about the dangers. After I arrived at his house and he listened to my story he gave me a ride to my car being fixed a couple more miles away. The day turned out good. And you know what else I learned?"

"No, what?" Rocco had never heard a story like that. He was fascinated.

"This is like karma."

"Go on."

"We have the same birthday. I would have never known that had I not gone to see him. A year later or so I went back but he was in the fields out by the airport. I drove back in there and waited by his truck. He came to me and he had these special glasses on. They had microphones in front of the ears on the black frame so he could hear me speak. He was hard of hearing."

"That is when he told me. The whole experience told me we should speak truth, men deserve to know if they have fathered a baby, or taken part in the miracle of life. They experience the magic, the joy, much like mothers do. He wanted to hear my truth that I told him all about my mother. He had a daughter, a beautiful daughter. Maybe he was too old to do anything about it, too late for him. But possibly he received comfort or a little joy in knowing he had made a human being."

Rocco's eyes watered as he listened. Rachel, what an angel he thought.

9

Hurricane Prep

"Incredible story Rachel. Think about everything your mother overcame as a child. But that situation has been going on for centuries, for sure. I love the fact you and him had the same birthday and you were the one to find him and tell him the story before he died."

"The other side goes like this. My mom married my dad; his family was from Canada and England. No big stories except for grandpa. He had a famous cousin, a sixth cousin. But that is for a whole other day."

He smiled. "Why don't I do the dishes while you shower?"

"Sure." She went to the bedroom, made the bed, and tidied up her room, opening the blinds and fluffing the curtains. He cleaned up the kitchen and thought about her story. There was some heart ache in that. If her grandma had not kept the baby and raised it all by herself, well, Rachel would not be here. All of us are a miracle, hers just has confetti and balloons and champagne.

She had just gotten in the shower when she heard his voice. "May I join you, Rachel?"

She looked over at his perfectly naked body. What were they doing? It was strong, it was a beginning, but felt like they were in the middle of a big romance. Maybe they had perfect timing. She had heard of that. Right now, she would not think about it one more second. She felt a softness in her heart, a feeling of joy, and she liked him, quite a lot. Maybe this was one of those romances where people know right away. It does not take forever she had heard when two souls are soul mates or meant to be together.

"Come on in, cowboy, I mean pilot." She teased him and smiled. "You can clean my back where I cannot reach."

"Be glad to do that." Rocco soaped up her back and washed it well, she returned the favor and gave him a hug when she finished. They kissed with the water showering their bodies coming between them. This romantic interlude was not finished. This was too enjoyable, too much, and unbelievable. The heat was heavy and too consuming. Real life gets in the way sometimes when we get too busy just doing activities of daily living, or errands. This real life she liked, or loved.

*

The two of them sat on the sofa watching the weather channel while the kids were due home in about three hours. The hurricane was due around Friday, so six days away. It was to stay out to sea until it reached north Florida then turn inward north of Tampa. There was still a week of preparation time and Rachel was happy about that. She had a list for Patrick and Henry to do around the outside deck, pool area, and walkways. She had her grocery items and supplies to get, and she had made a small list for Xochi to do so she would not feel left out of the happenings. She learned that right away to include her no matter how small the deed.

"I will be going Rachel. I thank you again for the date. It was perfect. I hope you had as good a time as myself."

"I most certainly did. I really did. You have opened my eyes some for what I have been missing in life."

"Glad to be of service."

"Hey, that is funny."

"I am sorry I could not resist that line. It seemed appropriate and timely."

"You have made me feel very special. I love the attention, the plane ride, the brunch, and now our date, even the overnight. It just happened; we did not plan that one. And it is okay. We just moved faster after a long absence of dating. You said it had been a long time."

"I will call you. I will be busy with the plane and the runs for the weather service. It may be a week to two weeks or longer before we can see one another again. My grandmother will go to Atlanta. She does not want to be here for any big storm. She will take little Johnnie."

"Okay. I wish her well, a safe trip. I wish you success with the hurricane. I will be thinking about you." They hugged goodbye not knowing when they would see each other again. He held her tight. Then he was off. She made her way to the couch for a rest and to watch more hurricane news about what to do.

She called Henry's house and told his mother anytime she wanted to drop them off was fine. She asked her if she was ready for the storm? Her answer was she was always ready, that is how one lived down here with a business. She would keep a few extra supplies as she was a business and people always wanted emergency items.

Henry's mother said she would keep the boys one more night, they were all playing well together. But Xochi wants to see you. Was that, okay? She said sure if the kids wanted to.

Rachel called the hospital to see if they had all the units staffed and if she would be needed over the next two weeks. She was on standby as her new job would begin in two weeks after the hurricane. They had the units staffed but remain on call basis they told her, in case someone could not make it in, or the storm hit harder than expected.

Violet went to Georgia by car on Monday and took little Johnnie with her. They would stay with her sister for a week or two. Rocco made ready his plane and missions. Also, the helicopter rescue was on standby, he had two pilots and two doctors ready for travel. Rachel would not start for two weeks as she had an obligation at the hospital. Then the doctors he had would train her further with the pilots, one of them was leaving, so she would replace him and business would go on smoothly. That was the plan. Rachel would go to the store tomorrow on Tuesday, then the hurricane would come by about Friday. She hoped the store did not run out of supplies. Do not worry she told herself. The boys had finished off the to do list. The chairs were brought in to the garage from the pool deck and any tables as well. Potted plants were grouped together and placed more near the house. Laundry was completed. Flashlights, candles, lighters, and water bottles were in the kitchen. Extra batteries were in a drawer. Snacks and can foods were in the pantry just in case the electricity went out and one could not cook. Peanut butter and beans and chips might come in handy. She made her list and went to bed.

Rachel woke up when a little hand was tapping her shoulder. "Can I sleep with you?"

"Xochi, are you scared?"

"Yes, I am. I am thinking about the storm that is coming. Maybe I should stay in here until it is over."

"That would be fine. This is a very big bed and there is room for both of us. That way you will not worry."

"Thank you, momma."

"You are welcome. Your safety is important to me. And if we get scared, we will be scared together. Okay?"

"Okay. Scared together." Xochi had a habit of repeating what her new mother told her. Rachel supposed it was an affirmation, a learning tool.

The next day the boys who had returned were playing games in the living room and Xochi was playing with her dolls. She would take Xochi to Henry's mom for the duration of the storm while she watched Henry. Then Rachel went to the store. "I will be back in an hour."

*

Back to the beginning …

When she returned the boys had left her a note about

visiting a friend. They likely did not get the memo about the storm turning. There was still two or three days she thought. And they thought it was staying out to sea. She would make sure they were safe tomorrow because tonight they were with a friend. She was not sure they should be out in a boat tomorrow. For sure by Thursday no boating. The hurricane was confusing. How did it suddenly turn inward? Did a hurricane do those things? She thought it moved slowly. She was sure it was not like a tornado; it was bigger but slower in action.

She went and took a bath, all of it would be looked after tomorrow. Tonight was the peace before the storm, the calm. She meant the calm. That is when she thought of Rocco and he would be up in a plane with winds everywhere, strong winds. Hurricane winds. Flying right into the eye to measure everything about it. How brave. How wonderful. She had a Superman in her wings. Seriously, she thought a pilot had a tough job. A surgeon had a team but a pilot had 100 passengers or more, a team, a cockpit, and a big old jet to maneuver up in the sky and back down again. Amazing. She slept like a baby. As soon as she was up and dressed, she turned the television on to the weather channel to monitor the eminent hurricane that as of last night had turned inward. Where was this thing? Today was Wednesday and it was windy outside and the sky was cloudy with an occasional rain drop. She needed to contact the boys, to alert them about the change. Everyone must be on the same page with the same knowledge and direction of the hurricane is a must know.

Henry would know that this was important. He followed this kind of thing. She felt better because he had lived through these storms all his short life, but Patrick had not. She was not sure what Xochi had been exposed to. Xochi at first wanted to stay with her and sleep with her during the storm. Then Henry's mom said little Johnnie needed a playmate and asked if she would come and stay with them. The day before, day of and one day after she would go into the interior as it would be safer, then by two days after everyone would need supplies and she would return. That sounded like a plan. And Xochi said she would make sure Johnnie was not scared. Okay, that is a deal. She would be safe or maybe even safer away from the shore.

Patrick and Henry had taken a motorboat over to their friend's place and stayed the night. They slept in late and then got up for breakfast. The mother told them in the morning that they were leaving the island so their son would be going with them. What were you boys going to do? What does your mom expect you to do? Patrick said he would call his mom. He had texted her last night.

Patrick had his phone by his side at breakfast but missed Rachel's call. Later the boys were playing outside and he missed her call again. The family alerts the boys they are leaving soon and that they should get home as well. The dad does not want to leave them there but they promise to leave before it gets late. The bay is not rough yet and visibility was still good. The island was not told to evacuate but precautions were in place. The mom had told them to eat some sandwiches for lunch she had in the refrigerator. The family left to go to grandma's house. The boys, Patrick, and Henry, continued to play a game in the game room and then got the sandwiches to eat.

Time passed. Responsibility drifted. They thought they had two days yet.

10

Rebekah Turns

Patrick took a call from his mom. She had begun to get worried. He reassured her they would be back before dark. The bay was not rough yet; things were just kind of like before a typical rainstorm. Rachel told him the hurricane was turning and she was waiting for updates. It was to hit Friday through the weekend and slow when it hit the shore but now it was to come a day early, which meant maybe tomorrow. Patrick informed Henry of the call and that they should be home by dark unless the weather changed earlier. "Sounds like a plan, Patrick. Listen I have been in these hurricanes every year, everyone gets hyped and usually it is just a storm that lasts, like the wind never dies down, it only builds and stays and does not stop. You just wait it out, take cover, stay inside, and watch for a storm surge of water."

"You sound like you know. Has an eye of a hurricane ever come over your head?"

"Patrick, that just does not happen. Never. Just winds and rain and more rain and more wind."

"This will be my first so I say we plan to be home an hour before dark, just in case there is a change in the wind and Mother Nature does not go as planned."

"I like that idea. You are a planner. And you are smart,

great idea. Which means we have until 4:30-5:00 when we should leave. An hour to get back and an hour before sunset."

"Two more hours of game time. I will find some chips and drinks. She told us to help ourselves."

The boys played games in an interior room at their friend's house, oblivious to any changes outside. Also, Patrick forgot to charge up his phone. Henry did not have a care in the world, but he should have. He knew better than to put off decisions about safety. Nonetheless, he and Patrick had the game box all to themselves.

Meanwhile, not everyone received the news of the hurricane turning. Some folks had weathered storms, never leaving, and never getting bothered. They put out sand bags against doorways and sheltered inside as though it was a forced camping situation. They had their bar ready and stocked, snacks and food already prepared, extra ice, flashlights, and some even had a generator just for this experiment. Others had bought grocery items, worried some, called friends in other states, and in the end, left town to safer habitats. It went like this. What is one's temperament, capabilities, mental capacity for stress, history of previous hurricanes? How well informed one was? And how many of their friends were staying? Another factor pulled into the mix is if you are in a zone that must evacuate. The suggested evacuation zones were north of Tampa near rivers and coastlines. Tampa and below were on a watch basis. Mostly it was wind and water, then power outages. That is how one prepared and prayed.

Rachel said a little prayer, looked out at the ocean, and wondered if she should leave. Both her neighbors were staying, she would as well. Her beach house was mammoth, sturdy, built recently and had three levels so she could avoid water if needed. She closed the hurricane shudder on the second and third floor, except for one. She would do that one tomorrow, she wanted to see out to the ocean and what it was doing. She called Patrick again for reassurance about coming home. Should she have put her foot down more? She did, this whole thing was to pass them by, only stormy weather would come inland, not a real hurricane. Nobody's fault.

Rachel had talked with Patrick at one o'clock and given him the update. He promised her they would return before dark. She looked out at the ocean and noticed the waves seemed larger with bigger white caps on the ocean out and beyond. The tide had come up closer to the vegetation. However, that always happens in any storm. The water had never reached her beach house. Since she began living in it about two months ago. She tried to call Patrick again, now she was acting the worried mother. Definitely. No answer. She would try again in another hour until she reached him. This is what moms did right? They became diligent, worried, and worried some more. They became whatever was needed in a time of need. During a disaster, she would remain calm, for others, and during the waiting period she would plan what was needed. She went to the kitchen and laid out all the supplies like candles, lighters, drinks, a first aid kit. She looked at that and wondered what that would do? Nothing.

She got out ten rolls of paper towels, five bath towels and wash rags. Now that is more like it. A big job needs big supplies. She had hydrogen peroxide, that was good for everything, and tape and a splint for a major accident. She had a couple large cloth beach bags to take these supplies like to the neighbor's house if needed or out to the road or whatever. Four o'clock and no Patrick, no phone call. He said he would be back by dark. She considered dark to be seven as the sunset between seven and eight. If he planned it well then, he would leave by five o'clock. She decided not to worry anymore and put that aside. She played music, poured a glass of wine, and read a book that needed her total concentration.

Henry finally got up from the game he was playing to go to the bathroom. He noticed the kitchen clock said five o'clock. How come Patrick did not alert him? They needed to get going. He looked out the kitchen window. He saw wind moving the shrubs and tree limbs but the water still looked settled. Not too much action. But they best get going.

"Patrick, time for us to go to get home by dark. Your mom will be worried. Nurses always worry, they know too much. They have seen the worst."

"Henry, my phone stopped. I do not have the time. Do you?"

"The kitchen clock said five o'clock. I did not bring a phone."

"Five? We can do it. Yup, time to go. Let us fly!"

"We would be faster in a car, then again, sometimes they block the roads and turn people away for a certain period of time.”

“You mean they do not let them travel over to the areas where it might flood?”

“Bingo. But we will be on the water, so no flooding there unless it rains.”

Out the door they went quickly to the dock where their boat was tied up. The bay still did not seem wavy or too different. They did notice the boat was up closer to the dock but tides did that sort of thing every day two times a day. The other thing they did not notice was the current, a strong current had developed and over the next thirty minutes a mixture of tides, currents, ocean swells, and hurricane force winds would alter their destination and put them in immediate danger. No phones, life jackets yes, no supplies, no radio, a small runabout with a working motor, gasoline yes, one oar, buoys yes, no first aid kit, and two boys with wit and bravery but in over their heads. Henry’s momma would be mad and scold him, ground him, and make him come up with a plan so that this never happened again. He could see her face and finger pointed at him wondering who taught him to be so reckless. She was like that; she gave it to him no holds barred when it came to the ocean and safety and boating ways. Henry would have to worry about the consequences later, now is not the time when one had to forge a plan and make it work.

Rachel was sitting there in her beach house, mostly ready for the hurricane. She was watching television when the lights flickered but came back on. She heard a wind gust against the window. The sounds that begin and you know something is happening outside coming from Mother Nature. Her skin pricked and she became alert. Still, she reminded herself hurricanes come on slowly, meander mindlessly for a long time, then slowly retreat. Someone told her that is how they come and go. There was a lingering for days on end. At least she had electricity. She was thankful. She became busy. She pulled a pizza out and made it in her oven. She would indulge in a big comfort food tonight. She would save some for the boys.

Sarasota had prepared for the outer limits of the hurricane Rebekah with sand bags, safety, food supplies, emergency crews on standby, electrical companies prepped, hospitals staffed, etc. But they did not close the outer islands, only to visitors, and people left if they preferred. The storm was not supposed to do much, just a watch and wait, maybe there would be some flooding in the streets. Restaurants were not expecting to close early, just on Friday when the storm would come by the closest but out to sea. No one expected the storm to turn in so quickly, not even the weather stations. The hurricane was picking up water and making for a super soaker with high winds causing torrential impact. Where was the water coming from? Hour by hour everything changed.

Sarasota Bay swelled with rising water and currents were in overdrive, while Tampa Bay was emptying out, the Manatee River level dropped significantly. Warm water was flowing in the opposite direction, not out to sea as in tides but being moved by this massive hurricane growing by the minute. And collecting in its swirls. It wanted to come to shore, where would it land and who would it hit? This would not be noted as it was happening but in retrospect twenty-four hours later when it was too late for warnings.

Rachel ate a few pieces of pizza and a drank a couple glasses of wine. Where were the boys? She hoped safe and sound. She told herself to worry in the morning, there was still 48 hours before the hurricane would be close. She went to bed and slept. She said a prayer for Rocco who most likely was doing trips out over the ocean. Damn. What bravery! She had none of that.

Locals who were leaving had to sit in traffic over the bridges but at least they were in traffic to get over to the interior. Rush hour as well made it move slower. But by seven o'clock it was greatly dissipated. Maybe most were going to leave tomorrow, the others that left the state had departed days ago. This was locals who just wanted to be a little safer and go interior because the hurricane loses its power inland. They went to hotels, friends, and family homes.

By seven o'clock the hurricane weather service issued a warning. There would be more updates coming by nine o'clock. By then their planes would give a more detailed update. Significant changes were occurring out of the ordinary and with the sun down it was difficult to tell exactly the changes happening. Stay tuned. Rachel tried to stay up but she was tired, all the planning, the buying, her recent dates, and caring for her kids had wiped her out. Not to mention all the to do items for staying put for the massive storm. She fell asleep under her covers but set her phone for six am.

11
Henry and Patrick Return

Henry put himself in charge when they boarded the small craft, a Chris Craft, Sportster model 25' in length. His uncle's boat was his pride and joy, so Henry must be careful to return it in great shape. Someone had rented out the smaller boat that he used for all his escapades on the inner coastal. It was then he made the decision to use the nicer boat for him and Patrick. His uncle had said he could use it anytime, just take great care as it is more costly, and he is upgrading it with fancier radio equipment at this time, but it is insured. Patrick released the lines while Henry started up the motor. They worked in sync. By now the time was after six o'clock and the sky was looking dark over to the west. Henry could not see beyond the trees. They were sheltered in the inter coastal from the ocean. They had gone past Jewfish Key and other notable locations to their friends place more near the downtown area of Sarasota and now were returning. He headed south to follow along the path for which they had come. Just go back the same way and they would arrive in about an hour, tie up, and get out of the oncoming hurricane.

The plan that Henry formulated was to stay close to the outer island shore and run along that way. There would be less waves, less currents, and less boats over there. The sky was darkening and he noticed he did not see other boats out. What is up with that? That is the biggest thing he noted. No boats. About that time for which he paid attention to he glanced over at the intercoastal shore, the waterline was way up almost over the bank. What happened in the last 24 hours since they came? The storm was not due for two more days. Maybe his timeline was mixed up. Patrick's phone was out of power so they could not check the weather. His own mother took his phone and was getting him a new one. His boat's radio was being replaced. The new one would be inserted next week. That item and the navigation tools were being upgraded, so he would be using his eyes to find their way. He knew all that and the intercoastal was not difficult to navigate.

Over the next 15 minutes or so Henry saw the weather changing drastically. He pondered if they should just dock it anywhere as it was becoming difficult to see. He thought he could see Jewfish Key, the island that stuck out in the intercoastal but the line of land was becoming dim. Wind had picked up significantly, so much so that his boat was being swayed towards the east. That he could tell. He tried to stay steady and keep the direction south but items were being displaced with rain, wind, and he noticed his boat tipping to one side from the wind.

The Bay had become choppy. He now saw whitecaps in the Bay. Whitecaps? One never sees that except from other boats and their wakes. He did not predict that he would lose sight for land until it happened. Their boat was being tossed about.

What on earth? That is when Patrick retrieved the life jackets and told Henry to put one on. Henry complied, as did Patrick obey his own idea. "Henry, we can not go far because we are between two lands so we will be just fine."

Henry looked at his friend through the terrible weather that descended upon them in this boat. Bad weather on water always seemed worse than on land. And right now, it was proving to be just that. Henry was not worried but he looked at his friend who just said the most calming thing ever. "Patrick, you are good in a storm. A beacon, a pillar, a light and just plain calm. We will be fine, I think. But Mother Nature roars like a lion and travels like a cheetah, or even like a falcon at diving speed for prey."

Patrick looked at his friend and realized they were getting into trouble. They had their life jackets on, were in a good size boat, without radio or navigation, and land was near on each side, but the boat was getting hit with waves the size of ocean hits, and vision was near to invisible. They could not even see in front of them. And they most certainly did not know that the ocean and hurricane were bringing more water to them than ever deemed possible. This was happening before their very eyes and they were in a boat. The weather service had not given the update yet, that was due in a about an hour or so. The current had dramatically shifted. What usually had water going out of the river and back in, according to the tides one could see this when near it, or by the smaller bridges that connected the islands one could see the water and which way the tide was rolling. But now the water was coming in and moving south, raising up the intercoastal sea level and moving south. Henry's boat did not seem to go where he wanted it to, and now, he did not even know which way to point it. He turned the engine down to float some and see where this was going to take them. Maybe it would move them over to the other shore and they could find a place to tie up and get onto land.

For an hour or more the boys stayed put in their boat and wondered where they were. Sooner or later, they thought, land would reach out to them. They would just run right into it. But it did not happen. It was dark, there was no sun. Just wind, lots of constant wind. And some rain, it came in spurts. They kept a watchful eye out the sides of the boat and both ends. Could they last all night like this? It was a dizzying sight and overwhelming to the young seamen. Henry kept the boat motoring at a very low speed, he determined he needed to go very slow in case something was right in front of them like another boat, a tree, or land or a channel marker. This was his best tactic he could accommodate and worry about the vocal lashing his mother would give him. Maybe she would just be glad he was alive and not dead from drowning.

All at once the boat almost capsized to their port side, a huge splash of water or wave came inside the boat when it returned to a level position. This scenario would go on and on for over an hour, or was it two hours? The boys were getting tired. And wet.

Someone in their home next to a park near the airport was up in their second level and studying the bay. They thought they saw a boat rocking to and fro. It was just a glimpse but more than the rocking they saw it move out of view rapidly like it was being carried away. Sarasota Bay was rising, faster than anyone knew. Most residents who stayed were awaiting the nine o'clock report. That was one hour away. This resident had a momentary view of a boat which then slipped away. It was close to the shore as visibility was only about 50 feet at times, maybe 75 for a second or two. It was dark. There was a mixture of sea, rain, waves, and low clouds which disturbed the vision. This resident waited for the nine o'clock report. There was nothing anyone could do right now. He hoped they found land and got off that boat.

"Eventually Patrick we must hit land. I know we are not out in the ocean."

"I agree with you there."

"What did you say?" Henry shouted.

"I agree with you there." Patrick shouted back.

Patrick was calm but had a raised alert tension building in him. Something was very wrong and he feared the worst was not over. Was he right? His sixth sense was spiked.

"I promise I will get us home Patrick. On my honor we will do this. We will get home."

Patrick was not sure what he was spewing but maybe he had to make himself braver than he was. Henry was already the bravest dude around and he really did care and was helpful. But now he was going beyond like everything was his responsibility. That was his Henry. He took responsibility. He knew they did the wrong thing by not leaving earlier, instead playing games not checking the weather, or leaving when the family left. He had done wrong and now he wanted to proclaim he would fix it. Right in the middle of a storm, he was going to fix it. But how?

Well, Patrick supposed that is the very first part of bravery, owning up to one's faults, and loudly stating you will do the right thing going forward. He thought about that, someone else would just cower right now, maybe even start crying or think they will not make it back alive. But Henry kept a vigil of looking, strengthening his resolve and fortitude. He would indeed need it this night. The terror had just begun to strike. The worst was yet to come and they did not know it. Patrick had had enough. He decided to lay down on a cushion and close his eyes. He would leave his fearless leader in charge, then wake up when Henry had them to shore.

At one point when Henry thought this wind might let up it did not. It picked up. What on earth? He could have sworn in all his young life this had never occurred. The intercoastal had never been this stormy. Why now? Why today, or this night he asked. He could not have known a storm; a hurricane this size would turn quickly and swell the intercoastal with excess water. He looked at his friend laying on the cushions after an excruciating few hours of turbulence and he made a vow he would get them home. Alive. He was not sure about injuries because he now realized the worst was still to come. They were drifting but not in a slow way. They were being taken away, swept away swiftly by a rising tide. Henry shook his head, he did not know what was causing this enormous swelling in the bay.

Downtown Sarasota was experiencing the flooding, a rising swell in the bay. They decided to close the bridge at ten o'clock and put this information out over social media, the news, and patrol cops downtown. The streets were empty, just a rare car by nine o'clock. People were at home waiting for the news report. Persons living on the Manatee River who happened to be looking outside or giving their dog a walk noticed the river was very low. Where was all the water? Other dock areas had almost a dry bed, the bottom was exposed, that was a first. Peculiar, yes, very strange indeed. People took pictures of this strangeness. Was there some sort of vortex going on, something magnetic, a pull? Whatever it was it had never happened. Most who lived around there had never seen the river empty or the bay above in Tampa go down. They would find out and see all the pictures on social media in the following days. Right now, though, they were in it.

Henry calculated that it should not take but an hour or hour and a half to drift to the land side of the intercoastal, but there were several factors effecting their location. Maybe they were swirling in circles. But eventually they would have to hit land, unless they had gone out in the ocean. No way. He for sure felt that was not even possible. They could be near the river or out in Tampa Bay. That thought made him go crazy. It would be rougher with more currents out there and the big Skyway Bridge was monstrous. He breathed heavy and let out a sigh.

12

Rough and Ready Goes for a Spin

Rocco went up in his borrowed plane at seven pm sharp. He would fly around and through the hurricane to record numerous measurements. He always remained calm during these exercises but did realize he could possibly get shook up a bit. This measurement was the ultimate in importance because when you had nightfall coming, people wanted to go to sleep and feel like they did what they could to prepare. Fearful they might not wake up and realize the danger, he needed to get proper samples of wind speed and direction among others.

Rocco had another pilot with him tonight. They wanted to be up and over the hurricane and then return through it. The two of them worked in sync as they had done this many times before. They sent pictures of their graphs to the weather station nearby in Tampa every ten minutes or so. It was an amazing event to see the hurricane from above, truly remarkable. For this one it was noted to have a wider eye and extremely vast circumference.

Tonight, they would also record after the previous five-day path that an abrupt change had occurred. It was turning inward earlier than expected. Why? Why the sudden change? What was the cause? Were the temperatures so much lower than normal? Was it losing its cool, like charge and just wanting to empty out its contents onto unsuspecting citizens and land areas?

Hurricane Rebekah wanted to make a change and come onto land sooner than expected. Mother Nature was acting up and these pilots were about to find out just where she intended to land. Rocco flew over Tampa Bay and could see that the water level seemed to be lower, same thing with the Manatee River. The gauges he had in the plane and digital maps showed the levels were distorted. He looked out the window. Visibility was low but one could see land. Hard to interpret he kept flying out, way, way out. He would fly back through the eye on the return.

After about thirty to forty minutes in the air and well over the hurricane outer bandwidths Rocco turned the plane one hundred and eighty degrees. Both noted that in the last 45" Rebekah had stopped going north. They saw an arch, a notable arch, and it apparently was a ninety-degree turn. Unusual. What was the pull? Was it the moisture in the formation? Could it no longer stay above the water and sought an easier landfall? What gives? Maybe it would turn and then go straight up the coast. Hurricanes do like to do that in some cases. But this turn could cause unsuspecting citizens mayhem and no time to evacuate or leave or prepare.

The recordings were sent in to the hurricane weather station. The hurricane was still slow moving, so maybe with this new information they could get the word out to inform the public to be ready in this new direction. This new direction went over the Sarasota Bay, maybe a little south of that. Well, thought Rocco, that is exactly where Rachel lives in the beach house on the outer islands, the barrier islands. The time was 7:50 pm and he and his pilot would likely be back at the airport by 8:30 or 9:00pm. He would be in the hangar by around 9:30. He would call her then and alert her. The storm might hit around one in the morning and last around eight to ten hours with the eye calming things down for an hour or less. It would be a rough night with outer bands on each side east and west causing wind damage and danger. But by tomorrow night and the next morning everything would be calm. A hurricane came and went and it pounded for over 24 hours but then it dissipated, especially when it hit land. But the waiting and watching for what it might do could make one go crazy. Hurricanes were relentless.

And, of course, the possible flooding from the ocean could impact the roads and homes along the barrier islands. Even bridges could get wiped, damaged, destroyed, and all the freestanding boats were like children's little play toys in the bathtub. Before he plowed back and into the hurricane, Rocco checked with his copilot, and momentarily chatted with him. "Manny, you got any family still in town?"

"Just me, Rocco. What about you?"

"Violet left a few days ago, she went to Atlanta. Should be safe there, I reckon."

"They will get some rain and wind but be fine, should be anyhow."

"My new employee Rachel and her kids are still in town.

In fact, they are over on the barrier islands which could get a lot of water coming in especially now that this thing is turning. I am going to alert her when we land.”

“New employee? Good. When does she start?”

“Two weeks. She is well qualified and you are going to like her.”

“Great. But I am taken. How about you?”

“Funny thing is we hit it off. We have been on a couple dates now, ah, make that four dates.”

Rocco flashed him a smile, in the middle of this hurricane and right before they headed for the eye. His copilot fist bumped him in a gesture of support. “Good for you, now I cannot wait to meet her.”

Rocco continued smiling until it was time. He lowered their altitude and business of flying got serious inside the plane. Concentration, togetherness, and diligence occupied the interior of Rough and Ready while stormy weather with a Cat 4 raged outside the plane. This heightened difference put the pilots on auto divergence, they must work as a team but independently minded pursuing the best possible outcome for the plane, knowing if one sees something different, he must react for the best outcome. “Here we go,” whispered Rocco.

Rocco flew the plane as steadily as he was able and that was a huge overstatement. They were used to the rushes and constant pull on the plane but tried to do as they had been trained. After a while the inner circle would really test their hands and fortitude but then a calm would emerge when they flew through the eye. Such peace with turbulence all around them showed them how tough Mother Nature could be. More recordings were sent off to the station for their report tonight.

Rocco and the copilot would do one more flight tonight as the hurricane trajectory showed a definite direction shift and a line towards shore. Once over land they did not fly through anymore. It would soften, be less violent and for the safety of those on the ground they would be done. He estimated a flight around 1am until 2am would work. Did Manny agree? Yes, sounds good. He wondered if they could get any sleep between these flights, or should they even try?

The pilots finished flying through the storm and quickly accelerated speed to get to his airport.

"Maybe we do a south to north flight at 1am, due to the turn it may come in faster and we should be prepared for that."

"Just what I was thinking Rocco. You read my mind."

He spotted his place, although blurry from rain and wind but still able to view. He placed the plane low and in he went for the runway. Gliding and breaking with the tires he landed Rough and Ready. Then he taxied her to the hangar. He thought to keep her out of the weather just in case something blew in. The pilots descended the stairs and made their way around the hangar.

"I can make us a cheeseburger if you like."

"Love it. Are you sure?"

"Pour us some apple juice, we will save the coke or coffee for later."

Manny made them drinks, put some corn chips in a couple

bowls, and set them on the coffee table. Rocco took off his boots and put his feet up. This would be a long night. He wanted to call Rachel, though, she might hear the news and be alerted. But he wanted it to come from him.

He made the call and was glad to hear her voice. She thanked him for the alert and change of direction, though, still uncertain when it would hit. She would likely stay as her beach home was far from the ocean. But she had not heard from the boys. She felt like they were okay at their friend's home but waited for Patrick's call. He said goodnight to her, she the same.

"I think we should try and sleep, just doze off maybe."

*

The weather station on the ground was a flutter with disturbing reports coming in from local businesses, boaters, people living along the water's edge all over the counties from Tampa to Sarasota. The persons answering the phone lines could not believe what they were hearing. The boss called an emergency meeting just ahead of the hurricane hunters plane report due by 8:30 pm. Just in time for the public announcement at 9 pm. At eight thirty a meeting was held in a conference room at the station. There were ten people in attendance: the boss and his assistant, two television reporters, two meteorologists, two phone service attendants, and two social media posters.

"At 8:25 the boss sat everyone down and told them "We

have five minutes to gather, get your information in front of you, and be ready to give me a one-minute detailed summary. At 8:30 we will go around the room one by one over ten minutes. My assistant will take the most note worthy items, conclude and prepare it for the on-air reporters. By 8:45 she sums it and gives the concise informational report to them and off they go to read, prepare and be on air at 9:00 pm. Got it?"

The two television reporters told what they had heard from either friends or family or other local news stations, the two meteorologists gave the hurricane hunters report of the noted arc and turn, wind speeds, eye center width, and rainfall, but the most harrowing news came from the calls into the station.

The eyes in the room stared in disbelief at what the service attendants were saying. Mouths opened and shock waves of disbelief were alarming.

"Oh my, I have never heard of that, I have never seen that."

"Where is all this water going? Out to sea?"

"Challenging question. Where is it?"

"Times up. Social Media number one go ahead."

The real panic set in when actual pictures in the dark began to be exposed. One by one she gave them what they wanted to see … actual proof for their very eyes.

"Oh, no."

"Good God! That is the bottom of the marina!"

The boss examined that picture and a look of disbelief came over him.

"The water and lack of it is the story. We might not know until tomorrow."

The final Social Media assistant confirmed with more photos. "One person near the Bay and the airport called in to say she saw a boat travel on the water as if it was being swept away rather quickly. She hoped they made it to shore. Visibility was scant if at all."

"Alert the police about that call, but I doubt anything can be done. But you never know."

At 8:46 the two reporters went to their chairs, got some makeup prep, read their notes, and prepped for 9pm. They gave a fifteen-minute update with analysis and prepared for the night. It would be a long night at the station. No one was leaving and no one was likely getting in.

13

Social Media Frenzy

Social Media was good for many things like keeping in touch with photos of loved ones, travel, lifestyle, businesses, and spreading information, even misinformation. For Floridians it especially helped during hurricane season which was from June until November. Because persons in the path needed to know for preparation or evacuation.

For preparation that meant hurricane shudders up, groceries and supplies gotten, batteries, and canned goods. Get ready for a party and hope for the best. If evacuating it meant leaving in plenty of time to not get stuck in traffic on the mass exodus and have a place to stay as hotels filled up. Which party were you?

Social Media helped to pinpoint and locate more sever weather. It was like the weather station had thousands of unpaid employees during a storm. It was useful. And in this case tonight people with boats were posting strange photos of rivers drying up over the last eight hours. What sort of supernatural power was having a gravitational pull on the water? Eerie.

So, posters sent their pictures to local news stations who gathered the information and kept track of this progress, confirming it with multiple persons from marinas, docks off the rivers, etc.

The mystery exploded and who better than a meteorologist to combine the information from the hurricane hunter plane and social media to formulate a possible explanation. A few bits of information about the saturation and speed of the hurricane would further help to speculate this phenomenon. The tide went out and out, then was partially pushed south and picked up by the hurricane itself causing it to turn sooner than expected and to flood unsuspecting areas even harder. The water poured in the bay through openings, or inlets, on the barrier islands connected by bridges for the locals and tourists.

And it poured in and in and swelled the bay like never before. The boys were caught up in this never-before-seen flood gate by Mother Nature posing a threat to the area. Swells, currents, and wind were accelerated by the flooding, a push and pull from the hurricane in its circular motion going out at sea, and soon to be coming in with a mighty thrust at the scenic shore.

At least people had their phones to text, and check in on family members and neighbors. Many persons were not so affected as they had weathered storm after storm after year after year. They had seen it all, they were brave, and kept their decisions fearless. Some had generators, some had parties, and some lit candles when the power went out. Some went to the interior bathroom and rested in the tub, waiting and wondering, if the house would explode, be torn apart, be nonexistent, or be flooded. If the power went out, then darkness descended with shudders closed over the windows one could not even see out let alone have light. If the fridge went hot, or the oven did not work, then get used to canned food or living out of a cooler until the ice melted. Many things go out when the power goes out for four to five days, or weeks. People realize then how grateful they are for the simple things in life like electricity, refrigeration, and cooking, or even showering.

The night was just beginning and it would be a long one for the people that stayed. They were not told to evacuate because the hurricane was to go north and hit the shore above Tampa. But Mother Nature had a different idea, she had a surprise in store that would be devastating for many. Especially two boys in a boat in the floodgates and a wrath so powerful they would see for themselves. Would they live to talk about it? Did anyone know where they were? They did not even know where *they* were.

Their friend who left with his parents was playing a game and heard how bad the weather had gotten and that the bay was rising. He told his parents. He tried to call his friends. His mother told him to tell his friends if they had not left, they should likely stay and go upstairs interiorly to wait out the hurricane. She was not even sure that was good advice, all she could think of was the rising storm tide would flood the place and winds would carry much away. Their friend tried to call them but no answer.

Meanwhile, Seth had decided to leave and go to a friend's apartment to the east of I-75. He thought it would be safer there than staying, especially if the power went out for days or a week or more. He and others must have thought the same thing. He got caught in a frenzy of traffic with the same idea. It was bumper to bumper and three lanes thick by the time he was close to I-75.

He got a call from Rachel. "Seth, are you staying or leaving?"

"Rachel, I just left and am stuck in traffic. You going to be alright?" Seth asked.

"I will try to not be scared but the wind is very much howling constantly, it does not let up. It just keeps coming and the rain is heavy." Rachel explained.

"The boys will keep you safe and grounded." Seth grounded her.

"The boys never came home. I am so frantic about them. There has been no contact. Patrick's battery must have died." Rachel's voice was frantic and high pitched.

"Oh no. But they are at a house, not out on the intercoastal, right?" Seth tried to calm her down.

"Right. I do not believe they would have tried to go via water anywhere." Rachel relaxed.

"Let us hope not." Seth said like a prayer.

*

The weather station repeated the earlier broadcast in case viewers had not seen it. It was too important and so every fifteen minutes for an hour and a half they broadcasted the same alert. The next fly through was to be around one am and two am. Then they would give a new update.

Out on the streets of downtown Sarasota the wind blew, the rain came down sideways and streets began to flood some, just enough to breach a few doorways but not soak anything down. Most places were closing after they heard the nine o'clock report. Patrons went home, either walked or drove before the final treachery of the hurricane would cause disaster. Hurricane Rebekah would turn out to be ferocious, quick, and quite a floodgate.

At the last minute since no one was home Rachel decided to go to Seth's downtown condo as it was a high-rise and would not be flooded. He told her to go there, do not stay on the outer islands. Stay by your phone as well, Patrick is liable to call. She did as she was told. She could not think straight. She packed a quick bag and took groceries with her. She would be close to the hospital if needed and away from the direct hit.

Seth got to his destination, safe and sound. Xochi and the family she was with were interior and safe. She kept a good eye on her little friend. Rachel made it thoroughly soaked but safe to Seth's high rise. The boys were nowhere to be found. Actually, no one really knew they were lost. And by this time, rescue did not operate to go and find you. They just could not be out in this hurricane with the winds so high. Persons who needed rescue would have to wait until morning when Rebekah passed by all the way. Rocco and Manny had one more trip tonight at around one am, or just before.

The waiting and more waiting were like a freak show in slow motion. The wind howled, the trees blew in one direction and it never let up. It was like these palm trees and live oaks were made just for these hurricanes with their floppy vegetation and resilience. Would it take off part of your house, bring down a tree, flip your car over, have it float away, or uproot all the signs in your neighborhood? Anything was possible.

More and more postings on social medias kept the person who sat in the dark or with candles alighted with pictures and news. They could private message how they were doing. Once the power went out then you would be in the dark. Later you could run your car and charge your phones battery. Better have a full tank of gas then. So many preparations for this big camping trip you were forced to take.

The darkened night with wet green palm trees blown violently and flapping endlessly about were strong and prepared by nature to take this beating. The television gave a view of the ocean from time to time with white and gray waves thrashing what little beach that was left as it disappeared from the rage. The brave reporters around town gave their updates and then retreated inside. Time would tell where the ravages of Rebekah would destroy or be saved by grace under this tremendous pressure.

The social media frenzy continued until persons felt to go to bed, wake up the next morning and see what happened. Rocco decided to call Rachel before his next trip out. He would wait some for now and then give her a call closer to the time he needed to leave. He wanted to make sure everything was alright. He guessed he cared about her. He wondered if she cared about him. Maybe it was too soon. A few thoughts crossed his mind thinking about her. The more he thought the more he seemed to care. He smiled. During this hurricane he cared about a girl, a woman, he had just met. He thought about his parents, they would like her he believed. In fact, he thought they would love her, just the kind of girl he should find and get married to because they were in the same line of work. He could hear them saying something like that. He agreed. And with that thought he smiled and fell asleep for a short nap. Manny was already sleeping.

There is something about a hurricane that quiets the night. Nothing else is of importance. It is the only thing that matters. Time stops except for the movement of this huge energetic being with a center, a center of peace. One wonders what makes this force so hard and consistent, so thoroughly mesmerizing you can hardly explain it. A cloud and rain make sense. Morning and night make sense. But a large glob of rain and wind traveling 100-120 mph in a circular fashion and then transversing over a course of hundreds of miles is like what on earth is this? Not to mention your house insurance does not cover hurricanes. What? I am telling you a neighbor says it takes a book to tell you all you need to know. If you do not want to read the book, go to Georgia and escape the storm.

Like Violet, she and little Johnie escaped to Georgia. They were safe and sound and would call Rocco tomorrow to make sure everything, including him, were safe and sound. They would get to hear all about the trips out and through the eye. Violet had already lost her only child and was not ready to part with her grandson or great grandson.

Rachel took a shower at Seth's and put a robe on with clothes set out nearby just in case she had to leave for something. She looked out the window towards the Bay but could not see a thing. She saw a glimmer of lights near the bridge that connected the downtown with the islands. Here she was by herself again. Another test. Can she do it alone? She saw a few people in the hallway so she was not alone tonight. That was somehow comforting. She then went to the bedroom and looked at that beautiful bed.

14

The Bahama Breeze

That is when she thought about her new boss. She liked Rocco and was glad he had hired her. She was happy they had a few dates, though she had never dated a doctor or resident, she would have if she had met one. The opportunity never presented itself. Her thoughts drifted to their four dates and the wonderful fact she would see him even more when she started work. It was going to be satisfying work, gratifying for her with her experience and more money for her family. All in all, a big win. She looked at the paintings on the wall, the curtains, plants, chairs and a table with a small sofa and television. The comforter was blues and greens with foliage tropical like and the four-poster walnut wood bed was inviting. She would sleep in here tonight, she only wished her new friend was with her. He said he was going to call before he went back out at one am. She imagined that might be around eleven. It was nine pm. She went and made herself a snack and a drink and brought it into the bedroom and sat over on the sofa.

Rachel snacked and then it being still so early she went over and laid upon the bed to take a nap. Soon she drifted off to sleep thinking about her grandmother back in the day and folks walking everywhere or using a horse. She thought about her mother raised by a single mother and thought, it is difficult now, it must have been very difficult back in the day. Her mother never talked about it. It seemed like she put it out of her head and forgot about it. Maybe that is a good coping mechanism. Just be forgetful. She imagined her grandmother meeting the farmer at the Red Barn, a dance hall in town. Even she had been there when she was young until they closed it. Dancing the night away meeting people. Who knew two could fall in love one night back in the day and maybe never see each other again? Sounds like a tale as old as time. Rachel supposed the girl who got pregnant must be have been mortified at first, relented, and then never told him. An all-around secret, except it shows, and later it cries. Rachel imagined gossip went around town until numerous people knew. Then maybe it faded away and was forgotten.

A baby was never a mistake in Rachel's eyes, she was a nurse, therefore a baby is a miracle. The fact we can live a long life makes it even more of a miracle. Truly a miracle sent from heaven with all the cherubs to be your angels. She was never changing her mind on that idea.

She imagined her mother growing up going to school, later becoming very pretty, and meeting her dad. He was a pilot and started a business with another man. The young family would have children but my mother would suffer a terrible loss. Her husband would die in a fiery plane crash, a tragedy, an accident in terrible weather in the mountains. Rachel did not know this but as she was remembering she breathed deeper and heavier, almost in pain, her new friend was a pilot too. How terrible for her mother with a young toddler and a baby in her womb. That baby would be born seven months later to a widowed wife, who now had two children and no husband. But grandma helped and made her mother's life easier by watching the kids.

She kept working at the crayon factory and one day met a man who was working on the train that passed by. He was a quiet man and came by often when she was on break. Their friendship, as a couple, would last almost fifty years. He became the grandpa we kids never had, the partner grandma deserved with help and support and love. And a father figure to my mom and a big help to grandma later in life so mother could care for her large family. It all worked out and blended well. I remember I was the lucky one, he latched onto me like a baby does to its mother. He adored me and gave me many things including money, toys, stuffed animals, trips to Cedar Point, Toledo, and Cleveland zoos, plus train rides. When I got older, I baked him cookies, brought perch dinners to them on Friday nights, devoting much of my time to them. I thought it was great, it was not a bother or a chore but a delight. I guess you could call that love.

Rachel woke up with a smile on her face and heard the roar of the wind outside, the windows or something rattled about. Maybe she should find the interior room in Seth's place. Instead, she went to the sofa and then answered her phone when it rang. It was eleven o'clock and it was Rocco.

"Rocco, are you alright?"

"Yes, Rachel, I am fine. Soon, Manny and I will go up for

our last flight tonight.”

“Okay, please be safe. That is all.”

“Darling, we will.”

“I will say a prayer for you two, and Rough and Ready.”

“Okay. Well, how are the boys holding out? Anyone scared?”

“The boys did not come home. I am assuming they are at their friend’s house and Patrick forgot to charge his phone.”

“That is a lot of assumptions.”

“Well, I did talk with the mother of the friend and she said they stayed back and are in their home on the island. She told them to go upstairs because of possible flooding.”

“Ok, that is better. You have an address and you should hear from them after a while.”

“There is only one small thing that crosses my mind.”

“What is that?” he asked.

“What if they went out in the boat and got caught up in the flooding I am hearing about?”

“I know your mind gets in touch with the worst scenarios, you are a mom, and a nurse, and now a rescue nurse. Say a prayer and quiet your mind. First thing in the morning we will go find them. I promise.”

“Ok. I will.”

“They are old enough to know better.”

“But they are boys with an adventurous spirit.” She knew it was a fifty-fifty proposition that they might have left and be in danger. She hoped not.

“Rachel, thanks for sharing that story the other night. I

kept thinking about it. It was rather touching. I want you to tell me more when we are together next. I would like to learn more about this grandmother.”

“Sure. I will.”

“Good. I will think happy thoughts of you while I embark upon this red baron journey up in the sky during a hurricane!”

“I will be waiting and I will bake you something for when its over. I am at Seth’s place as he is at a friend’s home. I am staying in the Bahama Breeze Room.”

“Oh, like being in the tropics with pineapple, watermelon, and an oasis of suntan oil and ocean music.”

“My, Rocco, you love the tropics like me.”

“Yes, I do.”

“Good, let us go there sometime.”

“When would you like to do that?”

“Soon, or maybe somewhere here on the mainland.”

“Anywhere sounds good.”

She heard in the background, “Rocco, its time to get going.”

“Time to travel, sweetheart. Talk to you tomorrow or the next day. Text me when you hear from the boys, or if I can help at all.”

“Will do.”

“Bye Rachel.”

“Bye Rocco.”

*

Rachel went to the kitchen and started baking. She was going to make a whole meal, refrigerate it, and serve it tomorrow to the hardworking boss of hers. She baked a quiche with ham and cheese, made a salad, baked blueberry muffins, made a lemon garlic chicken pasta, and a meat and cheese baked sandwich roll. Then she baked a chocolate cake with frosting. This took her about two hours. Rachel cleaned up and began to get tired. Maybe she would be able to sleep after all. Just then she heard a loud noise. It caused her to panic and jerk her extremities. It must have been a bird hitting a window or something, or maybe an outdoor chair moved around and hit someone's glass doors on another level. After she cleaned up, she set the table, less to do tomorrow she told herself. She made it look all fancy and special. She would be delighted to see her family and her new friend. She put all the prepared food in the fridge except the desserts, and went to bed.

Rachel only woke up once at around midnight. Her eyes opened and she stared at the ceiling and then over to the blinds on the window. She heard the wind howling and her body responded by a sense of anxiousness out of nowhere. She did not know what to make of it. Later in the morning an alarm went off in the Bahama Breeze Bedroom. Even then she did not know where the sound was coming from and walked around to find it. It was in the bathroom near the sink. One had to get up to stop it from ringing. She turned it off and went to find her phone. She would try to call Patrick again. Still there was no pick up. It just kept ringing. She saw that Rocco had texted but she wanted to get dressed and ready for the day before she responded. Get some coffee too. It was early yet, Seth's alarm clock said 5:30am. It was not even light out. Good she got up early, she would be prepared.

Meanwhile at eleven o'clock the night before the boys were still being tossed about, about an hour before they almost hit land and tried to see if they could disembark and make it safely. They missed the opportunity and remained steadfast on the buoyant boat with life preservers on. Their hair was a wet mop and faces slick with bay water. Patrick got up from the cushions he had been resting on and offered Henry a spot to rest. He told him he would keep guard. He would wake him if anything bad happened. He promised. Henry looked at his friend. He did need a little shut eye. He knew the storm would not last forever but all this tumbling around made him a bit seasick. Though, he knew once he laid down, he might become severely ill.

"Sure," he shouted. "I will."

Patrick changed places with his friend. It felt good to stand up after the small bout of dizziness. There was not much to do except look out for something big, like a yacht, or a steel piling, or a bridge. He suddenly remembered the intercoastal was made up of bridges. They had not yet encountered a bridge, or if they had they sure had passed under it without a hit or crash.

"Impossible. We must be close to something. I know we are not out in the ocean. It was just dark everywhere." He was talking to himself. His brain was trying to work. He guessed he had rested and now was energized.

Would this boat ever stop rocking? Would the rain ever dissipate? He wondered how long this storm or outer bands of the hurricane might last. He did not really know the weather down here in Florida, he had not lived here long enough yet. And now his friend had made a mistake, well, he figured he had made a mistake too. They needed to come out of this unscathed so they would not be banned from boating for their whole lifetime. As he talked to himself, the boat continued rocking, Henry slept, he looked ahead and thought he saw a glimmer of lights. He shook his head. Did he see something?

He saw an arch of lights above the water, high above. It must be a bridge. Which one?

15

Lights On the Bridge

Then they disappeared just like that. He thought he should wake up Henry. Should he? Patrick looked over at his best friend and saw that he was sleeping or seemed to be. He would not wake him yet until he knew where he was. For some reason Patrick became calm like he knew they would be alright, they would make it out of here. Was it a false sense of hope? Or was it knowing he had to steer the boat as he was in charge? He could not define the strength or false bravery at this moment of time. His life was perfect, he had a mom, a best friend, and a place to live. Everything in his life was great except this storm, this hurricane named Rebekah. He had been told the hurricane was headed north away from their spot, their home. But somehow, he did not believe that. He believed that maybe the hurricane had a mind of its own and he was in the middle of it. Even Henry knew better. As he sat there in the captain's chair of the borrowed boat, he just knew this is the hurricane. He also knew there was a beginning, a middle, and an end. The beginning Henry had told him is the worst, the longest part, then the middle was the eye and everything stopped, the light would shine through, followed by a shorter burst on the other side. Most people were inside during all of this. He and his best friend were in a boat, on the intercoastal, and could not see a thing. They were floating, or moving, around at Mother Nature's whim, a devil ride.

Right then Patrick looked at his wrist where he had placed Rocco's invention, a bracelet, on his left arm and pondered if this thing would work. Nice idea he thought. Maybe he should place it on the boat as the boat is going to keep floating. He would never know why in the middle of all this he took off his bracelet and put it around the shift or gear control for safe keeping. He also took off his life jacket and intended to put it back on. Everything was wet and dripping with water, he rubbed his eyes as if to dry them off. He stood up to try and get a glimpse of where they might be. Instead, he never saw what was right in front of him.

Patrick's head hit the top of the bridge and swung him to the left. In one fell swoop his body was hurled overboard. He exited the boat unknowingly via the port side. The thud and sudden slight movement startled Henry. He opened his eyes. He briefly looked at the captain's chair, unaware that Patrick's body went over the side. He closed his eyes again and began to drift off again when the boat hit something and stopped the movement. This time he looked again at the chair. Where was Patrick? He sat up and looked more around the boat.

"Patrick, where are you?"

Frantically, he got up and began to scope out the boat from stern to bow. He could not find his friend. The bow seemed to have hit something and stopped them.

"Patrick, where are you?" he shouted a second time.

Henry went to the front and looked everywhere. He could

see the water and then he saw a metal stair but the boat was rocking to and from. He pushed away from the metal before he thought to secure the boat. He first had to find his friend. He fell in the boat when he lost his footing. He climbed back up standing, searching, and shaking his head at the terrible situation he had put them in.

This time he made a quick plan. He must secure the boat, if only loosely, as Patrick must not be far away. He shouted for him again. No Patrick. He pulled out the line on the bow as the boat rocked again. The waves were coming and then going, the water was like an eddy you could not escape from. With the rain soaking him and blinding his eyes, his own tears streamed down his face unbeknownst to him. Pain scorched his face but his hands worked hard and fast. He pulled out the hook, his plan was to pull the boat and him to the stairs but each wave and swirl brought him close and then away again. Still, where was Patrick?

Dark blue-black water made this terrible dream a nightmare. Henry, he told himself, you were made for this. Think ahead of what to do. Secure the boat, prepare for search, then hopefully rescue, maintain stasis, or life. That is when it occurred to him, he and the boat were near the bridge. Which one?

Patrick had been knocked off the boat and fell right into the pitch-black treacherous sea. He was out, not breathing, floating down like when one jumps off a diving board doing a back flip. It knocked the wind out of him and he opened his eyes before he opened his mouth to breathe. He could not see anything. It was cold and dark and he felt lifeless. He realized after about ten seconds he was in the ocean underwater and sinking. He did not know how he got there but he must get out.

He needed air. He moved his arms and then felt a sense to move them above his head. He kept doing this until his head popped up above the water line in the bay. He heard his name and then he saw a big object, a boat come right at him. He turned away to get out of the way. He grabbed onto a metal rail attached to a cement block. But he could not get out of the way. He was frozen unable to move. He was out of energy. The boat hit his legs and body when it came towards the block, it came right down on top of his body and shoved him into the cement block. The grind happened so fast. He was the bumper between the boat and the cement. When he came back up, he grabbed the iron stairs with his hands and held on tight. He realized at that moment it was his boat. Henry must still be on board. He gasped for air as he had been pushed down under again.

"Henry. Henry. It is me. I am here. Help." He mustered out a few words.

Henry made his way to the bow. It seemed after hitting the cement block a couple times and the boat being pushed back, the closest area was the bow. He would hook up to the bow, then search for Patrick after he tied up. When Henry got to the front, he saw a head near the stairs and hands that held tight to the stairs.

"Patrick. Patrick," he shouted but it came out weak and

muddled.

"I am here. Buddy, get me out."

"Hold on. I will. Are you hurt?"

"Just get me on the boat." Patrick was turning pale. He did not know how bad that last hit from the boat was. In fact, he was not even feeling his legs right now. Only his clenched hands secured to the railing and he was breathing. He was alive. That he knew.

This is where his friend, Henry, turned into a savior. There was nothing left to do but save his friend. He secured the line to the railing away from his friend. He pushed the boat middle and back end, or stern, away from Patrick. Next up rescue, as the secure was complete, the search finished, and stasis remained. He moved quickly without thinking.

"Patrick, can you hold onto my back?"

"My hands are working but my legs are not. I cannot feel them."

"Patrick I am coming in the water for you; you will grab the life buoy, then my shoulders and hold on for your life. Understand?"

"Okay. Can you, do it?"

"It is the only way. Stay put, I will be there in two minutes."

Patrick rested his squeeze on the iron railing, he would need his arms to hold on to Henry to get on the boat, else he was, a goner. He could not even go there.

Henry still had his life jacket on but Patrick did not. Henry slipped his feet into Patrick's life jacket, pulled it up, grabbed a round life saver, and put the ladder down for the return. He went in and swam to Patrick. He had just enough time before the boat might swing back at them. He needed all his strength to board the boat with Henry on his back. He was not sure why he could not move his legs. They must have gotten hurt when he went overboard. And how did he go overboard? One task at a time he told himself.

He touched Patrick's head when he reached him.

"You are alive." He smiled at him.

"I am, Henry. I am so glad you woke up."

"Okay, here is what we are going to do. You hold onto this life buoy, the circle and I will tow you to the stern, where then you will grab my shoulders and not let go. I will climb up the ladder and lay you on the back cushion and assess the damages. Okay?"

"Henry, you are so smart. I will do as told." Fear spread across Patrick's face.

Henry swam while Patrick floated behind him. The boat was out of the way and not rushing him like earlier.

"Hold on. Hold on. Almost there."

Patrick did as he was told. He could not feel a thing except his hands holding the buoy. He remembered taking off his life jacket but he could not remember why he did that. It was when he stood up to set it aside that that is all he knew. Why did he take it off? He could have been at the bottom of the ocean by now. Where were they?

"We are here!" Henry shouted.

"Okay."

"Put your arms over my shoulders and grab onto the life

jacket. Hold on, do not let go.”

Patrick did what he was told. His eyes closed for a second. He felt light headed. He must stay awake. “Henry, talk to me buddy.”

Henry realized the situation might be even more grave. He had no idea what Patrick hit when he went into the water. But for certain he had his hands and some strength. Henry did not see another way to rescue his friend and bring him to safety or help.

“Patrick, you got this. You are going to use your strength when I tell you to, and relax when I tell you to do that. Alright?”

“Ready.”

Henry heard Patrick say ready and that would be the last words from his friend for a while. Now it was up to him to save him. Could he, do it? Of course, he could. There was no other way.

“Here we go, hold on tight until I say not to.” Henry took a deep breath and braced his hands for the climb to the top. The stern was quieter than the bow right now, so that was to their advantage, a small advantage.

He climbed up to have both feet on the bottom of the ladder, allowing Patrick to adjust himself for the climb.

Henry began talking to his friend to keep him awake. He started with the first time they met and hung out, then began about the trips to his special island. He went on to chat about the time they boarded the Coast Guard boat and should not have done that. Geez Henry, you need to be a better role model. That very second, he told his friend, "Patrick, I have done you wrong. I am going to do you better. I will not put us in these predicaments going forward. My mom always says to learn from your mistakes. I will not let us down. I promise to always have your back. You are my best friend and first mate."

He kept going, "And your mom is so sweet, she is the best. I am so glad you have her and now she is friends with a pilot. That will be our new adventure. Flying." As he said that last word he was at the top and he felt Patrick's hands let go as he laid him upon the back cushion.

16

Will Henry Make It?

Henry looked at his friend from head to toe. His eyes were closed and his face was pale looking even in the dark windy night. He was breathing. He thanked the heavens. Then he went down to his legs. Something was not right. His feet were not together. His right foot was limp and turned outward. So, he looked at his knee and thigh. That is when he saw a pool of blood. His knee was red soaked, scraped and an open wound with flesh torn about. But the blood was coming from above the knee.

Quickly Henry grabbed a towel they had in a bag they had brought with them. It was partially dry and partially bay soaked. He used it to draw up the blood oozing and spilling from above the knee. He lifted his shorts slightly up midway over the thigh to reveal what appeared to be bone coming through the skin. Oh Patrick, he said to himself, this is bad. One bone from hip to knee he told himself. He had broken the thigh bone or femur. It's like the largest bone in the body. No wonder the blood. But it was not bright red. Or was it? That is good he remembered. He had to stop the bleeding at the source and stabilize the femur, or leg. Especially, if he had to be moved. Henry looked around after he placed the towel at the open site on the outer thigh. He put mild pressure on there and held it tight for about ten minutes, then checked to see if it was still bleeding. It oozed out.

Henry went to the bag and found another towel. This time he wrapped it gently around the thigh a couple times without hardly moving his leg. His friend was apparently out of it and not having pain or feeling when Henry wrapped it. He put a shirt folded over and placed it under the towel to absorb the blood and have slight pressure on it. Patrick did not say a thing; he was out cold. He was not feeling his legs. Henry wondered if he should look at his back but how could he get to it? He wondered silently if he hit his back and that could be why he did not feel his legs. Henry had studied triage skills for paramedics online. He thought he should know these things. Make sure the injured is breathing, check for a pulse, stop the bleeding, support any trauma, move as little as possible, wake up now and then, get immediate help.

Patrick was breathing, his heart was working, Henry had just stopped the bleeding, so he needed to support any trauma and move as little as possible. The boat would not be stable after the eye came through, if this was the hurricane, and then the other side would be shorter but could toss them over board or sink. He looked around and saw the cement ledge that sits under the bridge near the land. It was about twenty feet from this rail that he had tied the boat up to. If he could get the boat over there and lift Patrick onto the cement ledge, it was the most stable area with the road overhead for coverage. He was certain the water had peaked. It looked like if he positioned the boat right next to the ledge, he could swiftly pull him over right onto it. And they could wait for help over there.

But first he would need to stabilize his legs, he wanted them to not be injured more during the move. And he still did not know if he had a back injury. There was nothing he could do about that except to minimize any further trauma. He would wake him up over on that ledge. That is when he got the idea for using the skim board. He went and retrieved that and brought it near him. He could log roll him onto it. Then Patrick could grab the edges and hold on while he pulled him over to the ledge. He would retie the boat and let out a long line. Then he would push off to send them over that way. The waves had let up but the water remained high for now. No telling when all this water would recede. He saw a railing over there as well. He would tie up the stern line and use that to move him off the boat. Once they were over there and secure, he would release the stern, let the boat float around until the water receded and he figured the boat might be close to the bottom of the railing stairs waiting for them after the storm.

Just in case Patrick was in shock he decided to take his pulse. He placed two fingers near his wrist and held them there. He could not count in the middle of the night but he felt that if anything his pulse was fast. Fast was not good but better than real slow he remembered. He might have been losing blood in the water for ten minutes or so, maybe longer. Henry became more alert and made the plan. He did not have time to waste. Likely he needed to get to a house and call for help. Though he did remember no one comes for you in a hurricane. Stupid Henry.

But this was the bridge that goes right downtown. A hospital was close by that he knew. There would be no helicopter rescue until after the second hit came through.

He checked his makeshift bandages. Some blood but not excessive. He went up to Patrick's face and felt his forehead, cool and wet. Skin, pale. Eyes, shut. He looked peaceful. He remembered that injured persons can still hear a voice. He got right next to his ears and spoke the best comforting words possible.

"Patrick, I bandaged you up and stopped the bleeding. You are going to make it. We are both going to make it out of this hurricane."

He waited for Patrick to open his eyes or say something. He did not. So, he went down to his ear again and spoke.

"Patrick, stupid Henry got us into this. I will get us out. I promise."

Henry looked down and Patrick moved his hand and touched Henry. That was it. He did not open hie eyes, or speak, but touched him and then his hand fell back again by his side.

This was a one man show now. Henry let a tear slide down his cheek. Then he went back to his friend's ear and said, "I am going to move us over to the cement ledge attached to the land about fifteen feet away. I got this. We will be safe there. I promise. I have a plan."

Henry went and grabbed two more towels on the boat in the compartment. They would need them especially if a rescue would not come until morning.

It was then Henry saw a bird fly in, a seagull, and circle around and land over on the small ledge near where the boat was tied. A bird. What did that mean? Henry thought. He stared at it.

Of course, it meant the eye was not far behind. He had heard birds traveled in the eye until they could escape and find another place to hide out. Birds are smart. Henry's plan would work; he took the seagull as an affirmation that this was the right plan. Thank you he whispered to the bird and gathered the items he would need until a rescue.

Henry remembered the sandwiches and snacks they had taken from the house. He would need energy. He saved a sandwich and a drink for his best friend just in case he came to and was hungry. He devoured the sandwich practically choking on his food. Then he washed it down in two gulps and sat there thinking. He made sure he had covered all the bases He would cover his friend to keep him warm and asses his parts for movement if he woke up. In the bag was Patrick's phone. Dead. That was a lesson learned. Never let your battery run down. Ever.

The bird flew over him and landed on the cement block and was joined by another bird. Two seagulls in the storm finding shelter. Maybe they were waiting for food from him. Maybe. Not now feathered friends. Another time.

Henry tore open a bag of chips and ate that too. He was mustering up his energy and thoughts to make this next move. Here they were under the bridge with protection from the rain, the wind had died just a little and the water seemed to be at peak. A couple of birds flying around them stirred his interest. He looked over to what he thought was south. He imagined exactly where they were. They were under the bridge on the south side. Their boat had maneuvered quite a distance out in the middle of the bay. He imagined they went in a giant loop, first south, swirling around, then east, and finally south to this bridge. As he looked, he saw a glimmer of white light on the bay. What? He looked up at the sky and saw the moon. There were clouds and movement but it was the moon, a full moon, lighting up the bay.

Actually, it was just beginning. Now he knew he had to get moving on the plan. But he would have some light to do this. He needed to roll Patrick towards the inside of the boat and not towards the stern side just incase he went to far forward. He would gently roll him and slip the skim board under his body including his head and then roll him back onto it. When he did that, he would look at his back for any cuts or tears. He wished he could secure him more to the board. If he could just put something around his core. Then he solved his own problem.

He took another extra line and pulled it through the side handles of the skim board and pulled it taught but not tight and tied him in. Patrick still did not wake up. At this point Henry felt like he was moving in slow motion. It had been a terribly long day. He would relax a little when he had them over on safe ground. One more task, then maybe he would go to a house and get more supplies like water or medicine, or gauze.

The shine on the bay became brighter as he put a few items in the bag and then he took a deep breath. He found the hook and pushed them off the post after retying the line allowing for the boat to swing across the fifteen feet. Then when they approached the other side, he tied up the stern to a railing and stairs over there. Once secure he talked to Patrick and said it is time to be on land my friend. The back of the boat, the cushions, were just about even with the cement. This plan should work. And he stepped off the boat and turned to retrieve his friend.

17

Henry Moves Patrick to Land

After Henry had tied up the stern he came back on board to gather the bag and a few cushions. He remembered those at the last minute. It would help to sit on those over on the cement. The rain had ceased and the center or eye was right over them. No Henry did not have radio-he just sensed it. It was quieter now, minimal rain, the wind was lazy and a calm prevailed everywhere. Even the birds were just relaxed. Perfect timing he thought. He checked his friend one last time and Henry could smell the blood, its odorous life of its own. It had a distinction and made you pay attention of its importance.

Time for action, Henry made a call to himself. He stepped off the boat and set the bag and a few cushions over away from the edge. Henry estimated the water under the bridge to be elevated by 12-15 feet. It was a guess; he could not be certain. He had never seen the water so high. Ever. Henry eyeballed the scenario before he grabbed the edge of the skim board, where Patrick's head lay, and began pulling it and him towards him. He did this in slow steady movements until the board was over on land. Henry's feet and calves were left as the skim board was not long enough. But he was supported so this did not interfere with him moving him.

He pulled the skim board all the way over to the inner workings under the road and as far away from the edge, just in case the water creeped up. Once done Henry went and seized any other life vests and rings from the boat. Again, just in case the bay rose again. Better safe than sorry. Boy, if he had to tie life jackets to the skim board, he was not sure that would hold. For a brief second, he imagined the two of them floating out on the bay with no boat and only a skim board, life preservers, and massive injuries. He did not think the universe would be that cruel. He looked at the birds.

Time to let the boat go and wander on its own leash. He did this and said, "Bon voyage, see you on the other side." He looked at the controls to make sure he had turned everything off. A little late for that now Henry and he saw the bracelet around the gear shift. Patrick's hurricane bracelet from Rocco. Ha, he wondered if it would work. Maybe if the boat floated out. Which he just speculated that the water that came in and filled up the bay would likely exit out from where it had come from. It most certainly would travel out that way before returning to its proper height.

Henry put some extra towels on his friend to keep him warm. He thought that best after the blood loss but he was not sure of any principle right now. His mind was a mess. What is next he thought? Take twenty minutes or so to forge the next plan. Do not rush. Think. Relax.

While Henry closed his eyes and recovered. Patrick was deep in sleep or was it a concussion? He knew Henry was taking care of him and doing all the work. He could not move anything right now. Even his eyes would not open. It was as though he was hypnotized or anesthetized.

He recalled his mother talking with a friend describing her grandparents. And so, Patrick deep in concussion dreamt about his mother's discussion with a friend. It was both soothing and a distinct memory.

Patrick over heard his mother Rachel talking. "I have so many memories of my grandparents, I swear they were my first family and my real family was second. I spent vast amounts of time there. I remember watching a guy named Mitch Miller on television. I also got to stay up late and watch Johnny Carson on tv. He was very funny. My grandmother adored him. They got to watch the movie stars of the day and entertainment folks like musicians, etc. And of course, we watched the Beatles on the Ed Sullivan show. "We got a really big show tonight," he would say. Grandma had all those newsprint magazines with sensational headlines from the paparazzi that followed everyone around who was important. And my grandpa read True Detective religiously. He used a magnifying glass to read it. He looked like a detective himself. He found money on the sidewalk and brought that back for me. He always gave me money, small amounts, mind you. But I remember when I was six, he gave me six silver dollars. I thought I had a treasure chest full of gold. He was kind to all my brothers and sisters but he just really liked me. I was his favorite.

As the years went on, I visited them every week sometimes twice a week and when I was old enough to drive, he bought me a car. Not at sixteen but at nineteen. One year he had me take him all the way down to southern Ohio where his former boss lived. He wanted to play checkers with him, drink whiskey, and reminisce about the good old days. I stayed right there for the day in the house. We would have breakfast on the way. I suppose he did me a favor by buying me a car and I did him a favor by taking him to visit old railroad buddies. He loved those days. We probably went there about four to five times over a couple years. I had a black Jeep back then and he even road in that bumpy CJ-5 vehicle. It was a four-hour trip there and four hours back. We talked and we had silence but mostly open farmland of Ohio. I do treasure those memories. I never forgot that kind gift he gave to me. It helped me to have transportation for jobs and to save money. I learned how to budget. One time after spending the day with them I was coming home and someone pulled out in front of me. It was a car with four adults who had been partying on a boat all day. I got out of the jeep to go see that they were okay. The car reeked of alcohol with beers cans, full and empty, rolling on the floor. They were a doctor and his wife. No one was charged. It caused me distress but it was not my fault. Someone could have been hurt worse, the couple was taken to the hospital with neck injuries but not fatal. I guess that is why they did not charge them. I learned that day it depends on who you are if you get charged or not for DUI. When they say most accidents happen less than ten miles from your home, it is true. That was about three miles away.

He took me to Cedar Point on the ferry boat and we came

home with cotton candy and a big teddy bear while grandma waited at home. Her legs had gotten bad and she could not walk as well. It was Multiple Sclerosis. She used a cane and then a walker later. Finally, she was bedridden which caused her bones to be very brittle. She called me Rachel Roo, a pet name. Except for a brief stint of two months in a nursing home she stayed in her own home all those years as an invalid. I think maybe that is why she lived so long in that delicate condition. My grandpa John died before her and she died a year and a half later. Those were sad times for me. I really felt the loss of those two. My world was shaken. She called me almost every week after I moved away. It was torment to be so far away. When my sister got married, we went to their house in the limousine so they could see us all dressed up.

As a nurse I signed up for the travelers' positions and worked for a company out of Malden, Massachusetts. When I worked in California John and I wrote letters back and forth and I kept those. Someday I will get them out and re read them. He had beautiful cursive writing. He made all the difference in my life like my grandmother did. I think they were my heavenly angels here on earth. One Christmas I bought them a manger scene from the local Hills Department Store. Every year they pulled it out and we could look at it. I think maybe we both craved the attention we gave to one another. Such a beautiful thing.

For a while after their deaths, I placed Christmas wreaths on the gravesites and talked with them when I made it back home. I guess because I had free time or I still wanted a connection to the past I looked upon the other grandfather not mentioned. I was the only connection because my grandmother's sister told me the whole story. So that is who I visited a few times, he was still farming out in the fields near the airport. I told my mom I met him but I was met with a blank stare-I guess she just could not face it after all these years. Too painful, I suppose. She kept it hidden, hidden away. And that is how old timers dealt with the pregnancy issue, with life issues. To shame anyone with a child born out of wedlock is weak and mean spirited. Yes, life would be perfect if it happened the right way but everyone is not perfect.

Patrick was still in his own little coma not feeling anything but dreaming. Then he felt a pinch of happiness sweep over him. He was sad his mother died but look at him now. He had a new mom and a best friend. She was a caring person, and a nurse, that was super special. Maybe she would find a husband someday. She deserved to have a nice guy, as nice as she is he thought. And then he stopped dreaming and remembering.

Henry was napping during the eye of the hurricane. He did not see the boat go out and out towards the bay and just float around. There were no other boats around and the waters were calm now. It was not going to hit anything. If Henry had to guess he supposed it was about two am. He opened his eyes and looked over at his friend. He guessed it to be about two am but was not sure of anything. Only that tomorrow would come and he prayed his friend made it to that day and beyond.

He thought he needed to go to surgery asap. He would call Miss Rachel from the house he would break into to get supplies, food, and drink, anesthesia (drinking alcohol) for Patrick.

Because he thought Patrick must be in shock that is why he is not feeling anything but once he wakes, he is going to be in tremendous amounts of pain and might need something to numb it. A bone sticking out of your thigh is not normal et all. He wanted to help his friend make it through.

18

Pain Pain Pain

Henry looked over at his friend and saw tears streaming from the corners of the outer edges of his eyes. Patrick opened his eyes and looked frightened. He began to gasp for air with a long intake and an expiratory cough. He did this over and over. What was happening? Henry did not know. But he got up and went to his side. He looked at him and held his hand and asked.

"Patrick, what is the matter? Are you okay?"

He shook his head from side to side.

"What can I do?"

"Oh," he screamed. Then he went silent and closed his eyes.

"What? What? Tell me."

"Oh, it hurts."

"What hurts Patrick? Tell me."

"Everything hurts."

Henry was trying to figure out what could hurt his friend after the accident was over an hour ago.

"Ouch. My leg hurts Henry. Is it still there?"

"Yes. Yes. You have your leg."

"I am dizzy Henry. I do not feel good."

"Patrick your leg hurts!"

"Yes, like it is terrible."

"I am so glad your leg hurts."

"Why Henry? Why?"

"Oh, because that means you can feel it. I did not know if you had a back injury."

He looked at Henry.

Patrick looked shocked. "Yes, I can feel the pain in my leg."

"Patrick, can you feel me touching your toes? Can you move your left foot a little?"

Patrick moved his left foot a little, and he said yes, that he could feel his toes.

"Patrick, do not move. And do not worry about the right foot right now. You have an injury to your thigh bone, so do not move it. We will get you to a hospital as soon as I can."

"Okay." He struggled to speak. "I believe you."

"So that I can make it happen very soon, I will need to go to a house, make a call, get supplies, and something to numb your pain."

"Yes, call my mom. I was dreaming of her."

"You were?"

"I will tell her that. Aww. What would she have you or me do right now?"

"Henry, you are in charge. She has faith in you for making the best decisions. You know that my friend. What do you think is best?"

"You are going to need surgery for the leg. I just know that. Next up, time is important. We must alert them of our location. I think they will send a helicopter because of the injury, or maybe a rescue ambulance over the bridge. Not sure. And keeping you safe and warm and checking your vital signs."

"You are so smart."

"No, stupid Henry caused this. But there is no time to weep about it now."

Patrick looked at him and dozed off again forgetting about the pain.

This time he dreamed he was on a train back in the old days like in a train that had sleeping compartments. He was laying down and could not move. He just looked out the window and saw grassy fields and trees with an occasional farmhouse.

Every now and then the door opened and someone asked how he was doing. He could not see who was sitting right next to him. He could not turn his head to look up. He only knew that he was being cared for and everything was going to turn out okay. He felt that. He could hear the moving train and the bells and whistles which occurred ever so often. He could even smell the perfume of the lady sitting next to him. She had a long dress on with brown leather boots. Her dress was a red green plaid with black velvet ribbons and her ankles were crossed in front of her. She must be his attendant or nurse. Maybe he was headed to the hospital where a doctor would do surgery on him and make him better. Though, he did not know what was wrong with him. He just knew he could not walk right now and if he let it the pain would surely kill him. So, he turned off his mind and dozed. The lights went out again.

Henry got up and walked around though the concrete ceiling was close to his head and he had to bend over up near where he had placed Patrick. He needed to go soon to a house while the eye was over them, else he might not have another moment and time would be wasted.

He was estimating how many minutes it might take to go there and back again. He felt it might take upwards of fifty minutes and the eye would last about that long, maybe longer. This storm though had been unpredictable. He guessed it turned in and wreaked havoc on a place unsuspecting and not as well prepared. He would try a garage door, sometimes those were able to be lifted if the electricity went out, or break a small window and climb in. He had a credit card on him so he could try that method his mom's friend taught him. He did not use these for nefarious reasons but in emergencies and this, this was probably the biggest emergency he had ever been in. He needed to save his friends life. He hoped the mothers would forgive them after they punished them.

He opened the bag of chips and looked at the seagulls, the pair was still there. He went and dropped a few chips. He designated them his guardian angles. He gave them a couple more chips and asked them to watch over his friend while he had to make a break during the eyeball and get back in time for the second show. The birds cocked their heads, listened, and made a few noises then took the chips.

If Henry had a partner, he would make that person stay with him. But he did not. He would be quick. He decided he needed to be thirty minutes maximum. He felt that an hour or two or three wasted and Patrick not getting to the hospital would be dreadful and maybe even a situation of life and death. The phone call was paramount, the food, drink and supplies crucial, and bandages were needed as well. He placed the bag closer to Patrick, looked around, checked the bleeding leg again and once everything looked like it was in order he spoke to Patrick.

"Patrick, not sure if you can hear me but I must go now to make a phone call for emergency services. They may not come right away but they will come as soon as they second show is complete."

Patrick did not flinch. No movement. The two birds were standing guard. Henry looked at them again. Then he looked out onto the water and their boat had floated out like he thought would happen. The water surge was over, now it was just standing still, waiting for the second side to blast away again. He paused and stood there looking for over a minute then quickly made haste.

Henry climbed around to the south and walked on more cement. It was wet but not slippery. He made it to a grassy area followed by stones and a parking lot for boaters and park enthusiasts. If their town had homeless, he would bet they might like this little enclave of cement and shelter. One did not even know it existed. But now Henry and Patrick did, unfortunately. And it was big enough to park the boat, get off and make a sheltered area for Patrick until help could arrive to get him to surgery for that bone protrusion. Patrick would probably faint if he knew his leg looked like that.

Once he had his footing he bolted for a group of houses off to the north side of the bridge. No one was out. Everything was dark. But the moon lit up through the eye. Perfect timing. Yes. He ran faster. He must get back as fast as possible. He wanted nothing to happen to his friend. He tried front doors, back doors, screen doors, and a few windows.

One house had a back lanai with a door. He tried the door. It was unlocked. Then he went to the sliding glass doors inside and they moved. He certainly hoped no one thought him trespassing and pulled a gun on him. He pushed that aside. Most people during a hurricane know to help one another and check on others. It is like storm hospitality. He swiftly went inside and scoured the place. He would have been in the dark, except there was a flashlight on the coffee table. He made his way into the kitchen and opened the fridge, took a few items, put them in a plastic bag, found some dry food, and loaded that in his large baggie. Then he found the pantry, he grabbed the paper towels and looked for a liquor cabinet. He found one on a bar cart. He took the plastic bottle of tequila. He would use the cap if needed to give him a swallow. He took the lime next to it. Henry did not dabble in liquor but he knew what it was as his uncle sold those items and he had learned all about it from him. Pretty soon he would be working at his store and needed to know everything, even if he was not allowed to bag it or touch it.

He made haste and was making is way through the sliding doors when he remembered the most important item. Make two phone calls. He called Rachel and left a message. He did not want to make her go crazy with worry but needed to sound like it was urgent. Then he called the emergency services: 911.

They took the information and said the services were down until the storm passed as they could not put their personnel in danger. It would be highlighted as a top priority. Henry understood. The time was two am according to the 911 operator.

"Bye," he said, and added "See you soon."

Henry took his two bags filled with items said sorry and left. He raced back to his friend as fast as he could. The eye seemed like it was almost over. Oh no, here comes the final show. He hoped the bridge stayed stable and nothing caved. He could not carry his friend to a house. He hoped for a bright morning with a rescue and trip to the hospital nearby. When he looked at the bay it seemed different again. The wind was beginning to stir things up again and his vision was being dismayed by movement. It cut into his eyes and pulled him in a direction he did not want to go.

Things were being shaken again. He wondered if they were safe? He figured there was about eight feet under the road if he moved Patrick away from the wall. They could either float or get in the boat. He did not like that idea. He could climb the steel railing and hold secure Patrick on the skim board for about six to nine feet before their air would be cut and drowning might occur. Because no way could he swim and pull Patrick in a storm surge to land. Three feet of rising water he could handle. Because their cement ledge was about four feet above the present tide or water surge height.

He made the plan if the storm surge came in, he and the skim board could wade in about six feet of water. He would hold on as he climbed the stairs and Patrick right next to him. It was going to be quick and over before you barely knew it happened.

Quiet your mind Henry, do not panic now, he said to himself. You have done all the hard stuff. Tears streamed down his face that he could not hold back. He wiped his face as the pair of birds flew back in after a circling out over the bay. They positioned themselves near Patrick and stood guard. Okay.

19

Boom

Boom. Just as Henry was about to go back in and be near his friend until the end a loud boom like an explosion or crash occurred and water hit Henry's eyes. He wiped them and saw, unbelievably, a car emerged and an opening in the bridge over their heads. He looked down, there was a wave of water coming right for Patrick.

Quickly he went to his friend who was still on the surfboard but had opened his eyes after the crash. He checked on him, he looked the same, pale but alive. He held his hand and reassured him he had supplies, had called 911 and his mother. He would take care of him in a minute.

"Patrick, a car has crashed from the highway. The highway bridge has fallen! I must check for a passenger. Be right back."

"Help them. I am here."

Henry walked carefully away from them towards the car under the opposite part of the highway where an opening existed from the exit lane off the island. The car was partially in water and on the highway on top of the cement. The front end was dangling off the edge. He went to the driver's side which faced him and he could see the person was at the steering wheel bent over maybe in shock.

Henry saw a dark blue sedan and an elderly man with gray

hair in the driver's seat. He went to the window and knocked lightly. Nothing. He reached for the door handle and pulled it open. It worked. Slowly he opened the car door. He did not want to startle the guy. He hoped he was not hurt or needed immediate attention. And he really hoped he was not having a heart attack!

The front of the car was over the edge but the door was able to open most of the way before hitting the crushed pavement. Henry reached for his shoulder to see if he would wake up. He had no further plan beyond that. Dear God, give me an idea. He looked over at Patrick. He had a best friend in need of immediate surgery and now an old man in need of his help.

It was then he thought, oh my, please do not let Patrick's side of the highway bridge crash down. Panic tried to set in but Henry did not allow such details to meddle with his plan of saving his friend. He looked back and forth from one to the other. Who needed more help? And do not forget about his own life. He should save himself. He looked up to the sky and the storm told him what he must do. The birds flew back in and sat perched over by Patrick. He knew what to do.

"Sir, are you okay?" He tapped his should again and the man opened his eyes. He looked out his front car window and then to Henry.

"Who are you?"

"Sir, you have had an accident. More like the bridge had an accident for you."

"Yes. The bridge. Where is it?"

"You sir, are under the bridge, or rather the bridge dropped you down here."

The old man tried to take it all in.

"I was leaving the island during the eye. Yes, I remember. I just live right over there and my wife is in the hospital and I thought I would get there and be safe with her."

"Yes, yes, that was your plan."

"You thought you would get there during the eye, right?"

"Yeah. Stupid, I know. But they do last a long time. Has the second hit come yet?"

"No. We are still under the eye. That is why everything remains quiet. But soon, it is going to roar up again. I must help you to be safe with us." Henry pointed to his friend Patrick. The man looked over at his friend. He looked at Henry and chuckled.

"You were stupid, too."

Henry smiled.

Now Henry went into Henry action. He assessed him quickly and quietly and asked him if he could exit the car. He though so. Carefully he helped him out of the car. "Is there anything in here you need for today?"

"That little lunch bag has all I need for the hospital to see my wife today."

Henry grabbed the red plaid lunch cooler and walked him slowly over to Patrick. He had decided all together was best. Because the storm could blow more items on the car and under the bridge they were protected best. Nobody would be driving on their side as for sure the road was closed exiting downtown. He placed him near Patrick and told him about Patrick's accident and the long boat ride they had in the storm surge. Then he told him he must attend to his friend, provide for him until he could get attention at the hospital. He required surgery but that could be hours away. He must give him something if he had more pain and must also recheck the bleeding.

"You seem to know what you are doing. Have you had some medical training?"

"A few courses here and there. I want to be in the Coast Guard someday so I try and learn as much as I can."

"Good for you."

"Does your neck hurt at all and can you see straight?"

"Yes, I can. Just shook up is all. My jaw is a little tight. Probably my teeth hit each other on the way down."

"I have called 911 and they will come as soon as the call is given to attend to casualties or injuries. They must wait until the second half is halfway through, they told me."

"I would estimate that to be thirty more minutes for the eye and say two to three hours after that. He looked at his watch. That puts us at four or five o'clock in the am."

"What time is it now?"

"It is 1:30 am."

"Thanks. Four hours or so and my friend should be in surgery getting fixed."

"What is your name?"

"I am Henry and this is Patrick. What is yours?"

"Nice to meet you two. I will say a prayer for your friend

and one for us. I am William, or Bill, Standiford and my wife's name is Grace. We have lived here a long time and usually leave for a hurricane but she was in the hospital so I stayed as well."

"Good to meet you. I am glad you came through that accident with no apparent injuries. I do not know what I was going to do. I suppose you would have had to stay in the car. Surely you could not have walked anywhere."

"Whatever you think is necessary kid. I can stay with your friend if you need to check on the bridge before Rebekah hits us again."

"Ouch, Henry it hurts. It is bad."

"Where Patrick?"

"My thigh and my shoulder."

"Your shoulder? Which one?"

"The right one."

"Patrick, you used your arms to grasp hold of me. I did not think you might be injured there."

Quickly, Henry thinking he is no doctor. Please God, no more injuries. He took a look and sure enough it did not look like a shoulder. It was twice the size it should be. Was he bleeding, or was a bone out of place? Maybe the whole thing was dislocated. That. Is It. It must be dislocated.

He felt it gently. He did not want to pop it back in and rupture something. "Patrick, they will take you to surgery as soon as they see you. Okay. That is four to five hours away. I am going to give you something to numb the pain. First up, though, are you thirsty?"

"Yes, I can drink something."

Henry gave him a red drink, one of those workout type fluids, he found at the house. They worked on that until it was almost gone. He needed that as he had lost a lot of blood Henry determined. Once he was hydrated, he asked him if he could take some tequila for the pain.

"I have never had tequila. But we did sip a margarita last year at a Christmas party when no one was looking. We did not really like it. But we tried to do the salt, lime thingy. I think it would help. So yes, give it to me."

Henry poured two shots in a little cup. He figured the only thing it would do is make him sleepy and forget about the pain. He knew Patrick was already being stoic. Just looking at his leg made Henry want to scream. After the first sip which burned some going down Henry sipped the medicine until it was gone. It tasted like strong cough medicine he decided.

"I do not know Henry, but I think you should be a doctor or a medic in the army."

Henry looked at the man and at his friend. God, he prayed for this nightmare to end. The lesson was done. He would not play with Mother Nature ever again.

After Patrick seemed to be drifting off, he whispered to him that he would rebandage his thigh, support his shoulder and keep him safe until help arrived. He also told him do not forget it may get loud and very windy when she hits again. He took clean paper towels and soaked them in water from a water bottle and rebandaged the right thigh. All he knew was keep it wet, not dry, and stop any bleeding. The shoulder he supported with a couple of dish towels under and beside it. He checked the old man; Mr. Standiford had rested himself against the cement wall near Patrick's head.

Soon it would be blowing and the water would be rising. Henry took a moment to estimate the water. He felt like the second hit would have less water, more wind action because it would be shorter. That was some relief. He positioned himself on the outer edge of his friend so he could keep watch on the bay and closed his eyes after he had a drink and a few more chips. Where were his birds? Thay had fled, maybe to a safer haven.

Patrick returned to his dream on the train. He had been on a train in Ohio before and gone to visit a zoo with his grandfather. He did not remember the train having compartments. But here he was going along and this nice lady was now giving him some pain medicine to drink followed by a plate of food. She fed him as his arms did not work. She was so nice. He told himself to thank her when he woke up. He wondered where he was going? It must be a good place because he felt very good. All the people were nice and extremely attentive. The train man knocked on the door and came in slightly making sure all was well. He said four more hours until we get to downtown. Henry never heard the town name as he fell asleep again into a deep sleep.

The old man looked over at his car before he too fell asleep. At least he thought, his wife would not be worried as he did not tell her he was coming. It was only about six or seven miles to the hospital. He almost made it. He was glad he ran into Henry who guided him over here. He might have wandered dazed and confused right into the water and plunged to his death. He felt safe with his new little friend. This kid was going to do good things. His heart was pure and he sure loved his friend.

The boat was out on the bay on the extended line. The bracelet surrounded the manual shift. Once the water receded the boat would come in under the highway, in theory, Henry reckoned.

20

Rocco Greets Rebekah's Eye

Rocco and his pilot friend prepared to go out again and check out the eye for one last run. Every weather station was a buzz and social media displayed pictures from those who stayed. They reported the water levels, winds disturbing the sturdy palms, and some had party pictures hunkered down with their neighbors. While most were concerned with their own homes, Rocco and his co pilot had to report the eye as it hovered over landfall. He had to report speeds, size, and water action when the eye opened the visuals. The hope is that it could help authorities down below with information regarding the areas hit hardest or prevent a catastrophe like bridges which may have collapsed.

The pilots readied 'Rough n Ready' for the last trip through Rebekah. "Which direction are we going to go? You have a plan, I am sure."

"We will go south towards downtown so we can see the bay and bridge, make sure it did not collapse, and then head west through the eye and check the bridges over on the islands. As it will be heading our way the trip will then be short and we will return by going north and around it to land back here. Sound good?"

"Sounds perfect. Let us go."

"We should return about three or 3:30, longer if it slowed or turns again."

The hardest part of this flight in the sky was the take off with sideways winds and rain or debris, but once up the rocking should dissipate. Rocco and his co pilot took off from his airport and as he did, he wondered where Rachel was. Was she still safe? And had she found the kids, the boys who went for a boat ride of all things. He knew Henry knew better but they were still young and unafraid. Rocco was glad his grandmother was in Georgia, safe and sound. When he got back, he would phone Rachel again and get an update.

The two pilots had their headphones on and microphones for talking to one another. They cruised south and made a turn westward while still over land about five miles from downtown. They hit the eye and it became easy breezy like the winds had parted just for them. It was like sailing only up in the sky. They relaxed. It was still night but one could see as the moon shone bright over the bay. He headed for the John Ringling Causeway Bridge. Downtown had lights but was darker than usual. Citizens had left and no cars were seen on the roads. Rocco lowered the plane in altitude while going through the eye. They would get a bird's eye view.

The Sarasota Bay was calm. He could see that. He flew near the bridge and over it. While he checked the bridge his partner looked over the bay. He was not looking for anything. Maybe a stranded boat, or one that got loose from the high water. Simultaneously they began talking to one another. They looked at one another.

"You first," said the copilot.

"The bridge has a collapse at the island connection. I think I see a car in the collapse," said Rocco. "Yes, I see a car on the collapse. We will report that immediately. What have you got?"

"I need you to fly north for just a moment. I see a reflective light in the water, no, it is on a small craft in the water."

Rocco turned the plane and swept around to the north so his partner could get a better view.

"What type of small craft. Can you tell?"

"Seems like it is floating about 20' from the bridge. It has a reflective light like a badge of some sort coming from the center of the boat."

Rocco reflected on his partners words. His mind twirled some and he dismissed a thought he was entertaining.

"Do you see anyone on the boat?"

"No, hard to tell. But I do see that it is tied by a line which goes under the bridge. Interesting. You do not suppose that is a distress signal of some sort?"

"Not sure. But since the two are very close to each other we will make note of it and report that as well. Now I am turning back towards the west. Get ready for the second show. Here we go."

They climbed back up and prepared for the ride.

*

Once the plane made it through, they had reached the outer bands out over the ocean, it became quite gentle again, comparatively so. When they reached this, they called in what they had seen and gave the updates on all the variables. Then Rocco made a turn north to return to the airstrip for a landing. For some reason he liked this business in the sky, flying around being in control of his whereabouts. It suited him and he had no idea why. Sure, he liked helping people but putting your own life in danger did not make sense. He casually brought up a conversation to his copilot. Why did he get into the business of flying?

"Why did I become a pilot?" He laughed at the question.

"What is so funny, may I ask?"

"I like going very fast and away from people."

"Away from people?" Rocco repeated.

"Like when you ride your bike as a kid and go super-fast, but then you have cars to deal with."

"Go on," said Rocco.

"I rode my bike everywhere, I mean I lived on that thing for about ten years, ya know."

"Yeah."

"One day my mom said, Thomas, you like being by yourself but someday you will have to have a career. Something that makes money. You love the outdoors go take flying lessons and see if that suites you. You will be surrounded by the great outdoors everywhere you go. And you can go very fast."

Rocco looked at him. He wondered why he liked it so much but had no explanation or reason.

"I suppose it is the freedom."

Now that made sense. Freedom.

"Freedom. Maybe that is why I like it so much. I think you just answered my own question."

The two pilots smiled and prepared for landing, this time coming in from the north with some second show winds. Manageable. The time was 3:30 in the morning. Rocco would put the plane in the hangar, snack on a sandwich from the fridge, drink a beer, and call Rachel. Then they would sleep on the sofas and go to their homes tomorrow. No more flying for a while. Time for rest and to catch up with friends.

Rocco pulled out a paper map and set it on the table when he was eating his sandwich followed by his IPA. He located the bridge, Rachel's island home, and the condo where she was temporarily staying. Something was nudging him. What was bugging him? He did not know. He did wonder where the boys were. What home were they at? It was somewhere on the island with a dock. Had they left there and returned? Or were they still out to sea or in the bay?

"Funny that a small craft should be tied up under the bridge, don't you think?"

"Yes. It could only be someone who got caught being stupid out in the storm."

"Stupid. Right."

"Very stupid."

"Kids are stupid or act dangerous sometimes not heeding the warnings. And that reflective light you saw, was it flashing or persistent?"

"Persistent, like a lightbulb turned on."

Rocco got up and went over to his work area. He opened his box of inventions and pulled out a bracelet with the special stones, or special light that shines at night when it is dark, kind of like a sun battery. He brought one over to his partner and showed him.

"I have been working on this for a while and I gave the boys a couple of bracelets to wear."

"And you think maybe I saw your solar bracelet on the water near the bridge?"

"Maybe?"

"Are the boys supposed to be in that general vicinity?"

"Thing is Rachel does not know where they are. They are lost. Stupidly lost."

"Wow."

"We called it in. But I am calling Rachel to let her know just in case it is them."

And with that the pilots toasted to a maybe, maybe they found the boys that were missing. And the bracelet helped in a small way. It sure did. The storm still had two more intense hours but it would be over soon. He hated to wake her up if she was sleeping but it was too important.

"Rachel."

"Rocco."

"Sorry if I woke you up. Are you safe?"

"I am safe. No problem. You must be safe as well. Good."

"I am. We just got back about a half hour ago."

"Good. Now I can really sleep. But I still do not know for

sure if the boys are safe. I have not heard from them.”

“I have something to tell you. It may not be accurate but maybe, just maybe, it is a good lead.”

“Okay.”

“When we flew over the Ringling Bridge, part of it has collapsed on the island side, the exit side. But more importantly, my partner spotted a reflective light coming from a small craft tied up under the bridge. It was out on a line about 20’ feet away from the bridge. It might be the boys I was thinking. I do not want to get your hopes up. It is a maybe. We reported it so the authorities will investigate it as soon as possible.”

Rachel went silent. Thoughts began racing in her head. What if it was? Would they be okay? Were they hurt, or dead? She closed her eyes.

“Rachel. It is a lead, a good one. If not them, then we will look for them later today.”

“Okay. I hope and pray they are okay.”

“If it is the boys, they are at an age where they think they are invincible, capable, yet reckless. I am sorry. We will find them.”

“I feel like maybe I should have done more, been more concerned or acted stern.”

“The storm turned, Rebekah caught many by surprise. It is no one’s fault, just Mother Nature performing her stormy behavior showing off to us humans.”

“Yes, I know about that. She is a tester.”

“The best thing to do is get some more rest, go back to

sleep, because you will need your wits and strength tomorrow. You will want to be in good form to rescue them and scold them."

She laughed lightly.

"You are right. Thank you, boss. You get some rest too."

"These hurricanes in paradise are not for the weak."

"Night."

"Night."

Rocco hung up the phone. He hoped he did the right thing. He did not want to alarm her but better safe than sorry and they could rule that out if it was a false alarm. He fell asleep fast on one of the sofas. Tomorrow would be calmer, except for the missing boys, and he would see Rachel again. That thought sent him dreaming.

Rachel walked around the condo, she had already cooked, set the table, and could not find anything more to do. So, she took a shower at four o'clock in the morning. She decided to get dressed for the day and lay on a sofa with her phone. She would be ready for anything. She said a quiet prayer for the boys and her heart. She would die for sure if something happened to her son or Henry. She loved both. They were quite a pair. Then she remembered how resilient Henry was.

21
Hospital Calls Rachel

At five AM Rachel's phone buzzed with a call. She woke, picked it up, saw that it was the hospital where she had worked. She did not even have time to think. She answered.

"Hello, this is Rachel."

"Rachel, this is Emily from the emergency services."

"Yes, hello."

"I have news to tell you. Do not be alarmed. I am the coordinator for the disaster relief for hurricane Rebekah. I am calling because we have had two calls related to you and your son Patrick."

"Oh my god! Have you found them?"

"We think so."

"Where are they? Are they hurt? Alive? Please say they are alive." Rachel stood and began pacing the floor around the sofa. She could not sit still.

"Let me tell you the plan. That is why I called. We do not know their condition, entirely. But here is what we are going to do."

"I am listening."

"First up, we received a call from 911 operators about two boys stuck under the Ringling Bridge. They were in a small craft and found refuge under the bridge. One of the boys,

Henry, made the 911 call from a home nearby. He gave them an assessment that both were alive but one, Patrick, was injured very badly.

Then we received a call from the weather services about a spotting of a small craft tied to the bridge. We have the exact location, especially with both reports."

"Okay, go on. What is the plan?"

"Engineers must assess the bridge before it can be reopened. This is for safety concerns since part of it has collapsed. I am sure you understand that mission. I know you are now in the rescue operations having worked here in the ICU.

I do not want to go into further detail and worry you, but Patrick will likely need immediate surgery." She paused, then continued. "He has a bone protrusion mid-thigh. Our operating room is getting prepared and the surgeon is on his way, as well as the team."

Rachel felt chilled to the bone. She shivered but did not speak.

"We will do everything to save his life. You must know this friend of his has done everything as best he could to save his life. We will get more details of the accident later.

They told me to tell you as soon as possible they will assess the bridge and run an ambulance or helicopter to the site. They estimate by 5:00 or 5:30 it will be safe if the bridge is sturdy. One part of the bridge collapsed and it is near them. The best thing to do is to come to the hospital when it is safe for you to travel and meet him there. I am so sorry to tell you this news but there is tremendous hope for all to still be alive and get here safely.”

“Alright.”

“They had no cell phones. He used a land line at one of the houses during the eye. He is treating his wounds as best he knows how. Pretty brave kid I tell you.”

“That is Henry, he thinks about others in perilous times.”

“We will be waiting for you near the emergency room.”

“I will be there soon.”

Rachel sat at the dining room table to gather her mind. She wanted to make sure she had things with her, and pondered if she should call anyone else? She did not want to call Rocco yet; he needed sleep after working last night. She would call him from the hospital. Later she would also call Henry’s mom, but maybe she already knew, or not. She would find out more. Was he hurt and did not know it? She had made a good brunch but it would not be eaten now, maybe tomorrow or tonight. How long would surgery take? She estimated in her mind. But she knew about all the abnormal things which could happen like bleeding, low blood pressure, even on a young person could cause shock, abnormal arrhythmias, strokes, etc. Rachel honey she told herself, not now. Think positive. Positive. Patrick was healthy, young and she loved him. Nothing like a tragedy to tear at you, open your heart, and bleed your emotions.

She went to the kitchen and made a small lunch for herself with a drink and packed a few snacks. She likely would be there all day and more. She said a soft prayer, made sure she had a charger cord, grabbed a jacket as hospitals can be so cold at times, checked her money and keys. She looked out a bathroom window that was not blocked to see what the wind was doing. Then she locked up and left for her car in the parking garage. She hoped the streets were back open.

The parking garage was a mess, full of wet palm leaves that did not last on the tree, other shrubbery, and debris of all sorts. Her car was there, wet, but intact. She opened the door and sat inside. Then she wept. She sobbed. She cried for Patrick and Henry, out there hurt, and cried for Rocco that he was home safe. She held herself in this moment. After a long pause she turned the music on. It played thankfully. And then she maneuvered to the hospital to face her own family, a catastrophe of sorts from a hurricane. Time would tell her the outcome.

*

Rachel parked her car and walked through the emergency room sliding doors. It was quiet. Only a couple people were in the waiting area. She went to the attendant and gave her her name and that Emily had called and said she would meet her here. The attendant seemed to acknowledge her and told her to go have a seat and someone would be with her. Then the attendant picked up a phone and talked with someone on the other end. Waiting was the game now. Rachel understood this and was patient. She placed her belongings on a chair next to her and pulled out her phone checking her charged status.

Plenty of battery juice. Good. Something was working during this horrific hurricane. The TV's were also working and filled with updates of all sorts, local and statewide. The hurricane still had to attack land and slow down doing less damage as it traveled its way inward. Tornadoes were spotted all over the vicinity in a certain mile radius. Mother Nature was quite powerful and persistent.

"Rachel Hansen." A woman called out and she walked towards her. Rachel stood and murmured a yes that did not speak. "Emily, we spoke on the phone." Rachel nodded again.

"Hi. I am so glad you could make it. I know you are a nurse, so you know how this works. But you are also the family and being both can be very trying. Let me tell you what is happening."

The woman sat down and had Rachel sit down too. "As soon as the bridge is evaluated, the medics will use the north side to go and retrieve the boys and bring them back over the bridge to the hospital. We should be getting the call about the bridge any moment. That is where things will be hectic and swift. There will be no time to waste.

Once they arrive, and if needed, he will go straight to surgery and the prep will be done right then and there, Xray's, IV's, medicine, intubation, etc. You understand the quickness?"

"I do. I can probably see him as he wheeled in, correct?"

"Absolutely, you will have a few moments, and then be updated throughout."

"Thank you. And thanks for the promptness and courtesy

of filling me in on everything.”

“We know you understand more than most visitors. You are one of us. All details will be given. Here is a consent form for treatment and surgery. The surgeon will visit you once he has seen the Xray’s and knows what needs to be done.”

Rachel read the procedure, possible procedure, and life saving measures that may be dispersed for Patrick. She signed it. Thanked her again and told her she would be right here.

“The operating rooms are directly above this floor, seeing how empty this is today you can stay right here. They have coffee for you over there if you need it.”

And just like that all was in order. Within the hour likely the boys would be coming through the ER doors. Rachel decided to make her calls now. Later she would be too worried to talk and maybe she needed someone here and what about Henry’s mother. She called her first. She answered and told Rachel the hospital had called her after the 911 call. She told Rachel she had been praying since that time for both boys. The two women talked some more and made a plan that one of them would be at the hospital over the next couple days to be with them.

Then she called Rocco and told him the news. He was relieved that the boys were both alive. She told him she had faith in this hospital and the doctors and nurses. He had the best chance of a complete recovery. He told her she was a great mother and that her new line of work was perfect, she was well suited to the business of saving lives. He told her how calm she was, caring, and a great health care worker and lifesaver. She told him how sweet he was and that it was more difficult to be concerned about your own loved one which made things messy. Her feelings as a mother got in the way, made for confusion and a feeling of being lost. But he made her feel better about that, made her feel stronger, and that she could pull through this too. He told her he would come to the hospital a little later. He was not sure if the roads would be passable or if stores would be open. He asked her if she wanted to stay with him instead of Seth's condo. She said she would after the first two days with the surgery and recovery it would be better if she was nearby. He agreed.

Then she called Seth. He answered and they spoke. She filled him in on the happenings due to Rebekah. He was shocked. Then she heard a female voice in the background ask, "What happened?"

"Seth, you are with someone." Rachel made a blanket statement. Rachel wondered if it was the one he had been talking about and dating.

"I am but it is somebody new."

"You are serious then, again. How many is this?"

"I have not found the right one."

"What is the right one? Was I the right one?"

"This dating thing is hard."

She knew she should not say it but she lost her mind temporarily and spit it out. "When you sleep with them, all of them, maybe they just want sex. Maybe you just want sex. I know, sex is great. But if you want love, well, wait a couple weeks and find out, maybe."

"You always know what is best. That is why I know I loved you. I am sorry we parted. We did do quite a mission. Good work Rachel."

"Good work Rachel?"

"Yes."

She laughed. "I can not hate you, but I cannot love you. You always need something new, something tasty, something fresh. But I am glad you are out of the nasty business of spying."

"Yeah, about that. Not quite. Think of it this way. I get the super bad guys but need extra support from beautiful women. And you are one of them."

"I do not know what to say to that. So, I will not say anything. But I will ask a favor of you."

"Ask away, I am here to help you."

"I met someone."

"Oh yeah?"

"Tall, dark and handsome."

"I am intrigued."

22

The Final Show —The Eye Passes.

The next two hours would be harrowing for the three underneath the bridge as they waited out the second hit from Rebekah.

All three momentarily slept beside one another as they braced for the storm to come over them. The strong winds came in bands lathering up gusts and tossing debris right next to them on both sides. They were protected from a direct hit but not the sounds of swirling and pushing forces from her might. The birds were long gone but no one underneath the bridge cared anymore. They only waited and waited. Henry had wrapped a blanket around him from Bill's car after he had tended to his mates. He sat up, he figured he needed to be ready but fell asleep like the others for a while with his head against the cement wall. He estimated right before he fell asleep it must be 3:00 or 3:30 as the eye was gone. A couple more hours he told himself before he dozed off. Patrick began stirring slightly in and out. While Bill was out.

It was dark like the night and only the wind made any noise. An occasional toss of debris made its way onto Bill's car and it became plastered with mostly foliage of many kinds. The wind howled down and through and with nowhere to go but past the three live bodies or down and away towards the city. A couple of large tree branches hit the car against the back window.

Then a pause of silence came before the next hit. It woke all three stranded below. They did not know what happened, but a sign had come loose and traveled likely at 100 miles per hour and smacked into the back window of the teetering car.

Suddenly glass spattered everywhere and flew like icicles landing and shattering in the winter time. The boys and Bill opened their eyes and were almost afraid to look around for getting hit with an unknown object. Loud sounds non stop and wind swept over them. Bill and Henry looked over at his car as it was swept up in the air. The back end lifted and pushed the vehicle over the cement ledge forcing steel to grate over cement and make a screeching noise that did not stop for over a minute. The sheer force kept beating it, lifting it, until finally it plunged into the water. Bill could not believe his eyes. He wiped them and looked again. Gone. Over. The Edge.

He stared ahead forward for a long space, then turned to look at Henry watching in disbelief.

He gave him a small salute and mustered out, "Henry, my son, you saved my life." Then he cried silently knowing he was blessed and would see his wife later.

At this point Henry was in disbelief. He did not know how he came to make that decision, God help him, but Henry became a little scared at this point. He tried to think about anything else he could do until they were rescued. Just then more wind, loud noises, and a feeling of dread poured over all of them. Henry and Bill covered their eyes; Patrick's were closed but he was not asleep. He had begun to feel more pain and he had to pee. He just had to go.

"Henry, I have to go to the bathroom." He whispered. His friend bent down over him and told him to repeat it.

"Sure, no problem. Go in this cup. I will help you."

"Ok."

"We want to keep the injury clear of your pee."

"Ok."

Henry took the cup and tossed the urine over the edge. He checked on his friend again and looked over at the old man. He sure hoped he did not have a heart attack as seniors can have that at any stressful moment. He knew CPR but this is not the place. This is not a hospital.

For a while things slowed down a bit, must be a band going through. That is how these hurricanes work, swift and deadly one minute, some slowing the next, thunderous after that, water surging, large objects floating and bridges collapsing.

When Henry figured this out, he got back up and checked on Bill's car. Yup it had sunk completely. It was completely submerged. Carefully he walked, slowly, and then he went to the north side to check on their boat. He wanted to see if it was still tied up. The water had risen but not all the way up like earlier. Where was all that water going, he pondered? He looked and looked.

That is when he looked at where he had tied up the boat. The line was floating but no boat attached. He looked out into the darkness, visibility was poor. Still no boat. Maybe it got taken away or disconnected. He followed the line all the way out past the cement ledge where it went under water. Did the boat sink? What? Maybe it toppled over, like the car that went over.

"Henry, everything okay?"

"Not sure. I think the boat is gone."

"Really?"

"Or it sunk." Henry began to realize this storm needed to end very soon before this ledge is no longer safe. Was there a third catastrophe waiting to happen? The thought sent him spiraling, but not in a bad way. He was sent into a state of super alertness. He went back to his mates.

"Guys."

"Yes, Henry." They said in unison.

"We have lost a car, and a boat, but the bridge still stands. We must pray for her and us."

"Sure, I can do that." Bill said a prayer for all of them, the bridge, and then thanked his captain for the excellent work he had done.

When it was finished, Patrick spoke up. "What's next Captain Henry?"

Henry figured it was now around five o'clock, or close to it. The rescue had to be coming around or close to six. Another hour of torment. What should they do?

"Oh, Henry, the pain is back. It is a stabbing pain in my leg. Ouch, aww man. Make it go away. Please." Patrick begged and cried.

"Do it Henry, give him one more shot for the pain. You know it has got to be killing him." Bill took pity on Patrick recognizing his distress.

"My mates and I shall have a shot of courage. Yes. That is, it. One for everyone as there is nothing left to lose."

Henry knew you were not supposed to eat or drink before surgery, but now it had been hours. One more shot will just make him sleep until they get here, then they will take care of everything. He listened to Patrick screaming and he relented. He took out three cups and poured all of them a taste and hand delivered it to Patrick, his mate lying down in extreme pain.

Bill took his and asked for another. Henry swallowed one and was done. He was in charge, after all, of these operations he concluded. The storm continued in bands coming and going and slowly dissipating in outrage. The three remained huddled, close by, weathering any further outbursts that might besiege them.

All three fell asleep and remained under cover for the next hour.

*

Back at the hospital Rachel was drinking coffee when the surgeon walked in and told her what to expect. He was an orthopedic surgeon and would fix Patrick as best he could, followed by rehabilitation, but a young person had every chance at a full recovery. Mostly he encountered auto mobile accidents or sports players getting these, even hikers falling from various heights. He would be on top of possible infections from the salt water or other dirt depending upon how the fracture occurred. It seemed though that his friend was keeping it wet and clean. He did wonder how bad the pain might be or if he was asleep. Soon. He told her. He had a team and general surgeon with him to handle any unsuspected injuries not seen yet. He told her just about a minute or two with him is all as he is wheeled down to the elevators. He was not sure he would even be awake. Then in recovery you can be with him right away. Yes. She knew that. She wished him luck and told him to take good care of her little Patrick. Henry might be injured too and not know it. He told her the ER would assess Henry. And there might be more persons whose car collapsed the bridge near them. They just did not know yet. Just then the surgeon got a call. He said, "This is the bridge people."

He turned and gave her a thumbs up. "The bridge is open for the rescue. Only the one side, the north side, right where they are."

Rachel smiled. She went and sat back down. Now comes the hard part. She prayed.

The next time she looked up at the television she saw an emergency vehicle, an ambulance was driving over the bridge headed to the island. The reporter stated a rescue was in place and that was all she knew. Stay tuned she said. Rachel became glued to the tv.

"The Ringling Bridge has been closed for over twenty-four hours as residents had exited and were not allowed back on. It is being said a partial collapse has occurred on the island side. But 911 reports indicate a rescue is in place for a couple boys caught in the storm surge. We will bring you more news as it comes in. We certainly hope all are well after Rebekah hit hard when she took a turn inward and surprised everyone. It was a rapid turn wreaking havoc on the island and surrounding areas. We will be on top of it all right here. Check back."

Rachel filled up her coffee cup and returned to her seat. She could see the television and the sliding doors out in front of her. She waited patiently.

Meanwhile, Seth got up and showered and told his girlfriend he was headed to the hospital. His friend, and previous partner, would need him. She had her hands filled with an injured son, a little daughter staying with someone else, and her residence was on the island. Maybe it was even flooded or something, he did not know. But he must go. It was the right thing to do to give her support during a critical time. She had made his mission complete and a success.

Rocco was worried about Rachel. And he missed her so much. He cleaned up his place. He called his grandmother and got the updates. He went to the store which had opened already and bought a few groceries. He had not planned that very well ahead of time. He checked his phone and played around a bit. He checked on places to stay in St. Augustine and found a couple he liked. He thought that Rachel and him should go there, a couple of resumes he received looked promising, and he wanted to meet them. And he wanted to ask Rachel a very important question.

He saved them to his emails. He was going to the hospital in a few hours to be with her, support her, and check on the boys. He turned on the television and saw some of the damage the hurricane had caused. He was still amazed his co pilot caught the light from the bracelet. The light emits better at night, so maybe when they were in the eye the boat was still covered in darkness. He speculated that to be what happened. Anyway, it was a good start. Of course, one had to have it and at the right time in the right circumstances. He wondered what else could it be used for? It was like a shining star only not in the sky.

23

Patrick Dreams the Final Show

Over the next hour Patrick began dreaming again. Or maybe he was hallucinating, he did not know. He only knew he was back on the train. But to where?

He opened his eyes. The train was moving as he could catch a glimpse of things passing by. He could not see the woman next to him but he could see her dress again. There was that black and red plaid, a dark burgundy and it covered her legs all the way to her black leather boots.

She began to talk to him and this comforted him. He wanted to ask her more questions like where were they going?

"Patrick, are you hungry?" She asked.

"Yes, I am. Where are we going to?"

"No need to worry about that yet. Let me feed you first and then we can talk. Sound good?"

She pulled a tray of food on a table closer to them.

"I cannot feed myself?"

"You are too weak, Patrick. A couple days ago you had surgery on your leg after a bad accident."

"Oh, I see. That is why I cannot move my legs."

"And your arm was dislocated so they fixed your shoulder. I gave you something for the pain, maybe that is why you are very sleepy. Are you comfortable?"

"Yes. Please give me some food. I will eat whatever you have."

She began to feed him and leaned over, then he got a better look at her. She looked familiar. He recognized her face. He thought he knew her. He kept eating he was so hungry. Still weak though he reckoned. Accident. He did not remember any accident. He had many questions. Maybe he would save them up and ask later. There was a knock on the door and a gentleman in a suit stepped inside and looked at Patrick and said hello. He looked familiar too. Who was he?

"Patrick, this is Mr. Sullivan, my husband."

"Husband?"

"Yes, we have recently been married. We are a family now."

"Family?"

"You do not remember the wedding?"

"Right now, I do not remember anything. Maybe you can tell me tomorrow all about it."

"You have been through quite a lot. You do remember that I am your mother, right?"

"Yes, ma'am. I thought you were."

"I will always be your mother, now and forever. Keep eating. This will all make sense tomorrow."

Patrick kept eating and she gave him a drink too. She was so kind and beautiful. He just did not know where he was or where he was going but he trusted her. He did everything she told him to do.

"Alright, I will let you two be and will return when it is time to sleep. We will be there tomorrow morning. Then all will be alright." The gentleman left and closed the door.

Patrick did not have the strength to ask him where it is they were going. He was done eating and drinking and his mother wiped his mouth for him. He looked at her when she leaned over to do this. He would like to give her a big hug but he could not move. He could not even move his arms. He felt like he was dead in his body. Maybe tomorrow he would have more strength and find out where they were going. He must be dreaming but she looked real and so did the gentleman. Who was he? Did he know him? Before he dozed off, he looked out the window again. This train was moving rather fast; the countryside was a blur. It went from grassy areas to houses and farms. The lady, his mother, got up and said she would be right back. She opened the door and he felt a big breeze sweep over him. She turned around and pulled up the blanket to cover him up. Then she leaned over and kissed him on the forehead and said, "I love you, Patrick."

He fell asleep before he could return the emotion back to her. But he smiled and felt all cozy and comfortable. Nothing hurt now. He felt good. Time passed. He had no cares or wants.

Time slowed over that last hour when there is nothing to do but wait knowing that someone was coming to save them. They felt it, fell asleep, woke, looked around, heard the noise of the howling wind, and closed their eyes again. Like a trance, each was in their own world.

Bill was thinking about his wife. He wanted to see her today. Soon she would be coming home. He was grateful for that. They had received good news and she could recuperate at home. He had fixed everything at home to make it easy for her. He would get her back on her feet and they could go on enjoying all the things, or maybe new things, that they might want to do. He planned on a cruise near Christmas time. He knew she would like that. He asked the kids and their grandchildren to join them for a big trip. He smiled. He had something to look forward to. They had all said yes, and it was a big surprise for his wife. He thought she might be thrilled with this. No, he knew she would. She liked it when they were all together. She would not have to cook or clean or do a darn thing. Joyous Noel indeed.

Henry let his mind wander and was having a talk with himself. Time to grow up Henry and take more responsibility. Leave that kid stuff behind. Soon he would be fifteen and getting his drivers permit. He had to be doing the right things and not getting into trouble in big storms and sneaking out at night in the boat. If he wanted to get into the Coast Guard, he had to act like he already was by improving his grades, respecting his mothers' rules, and following his elders' commands. Yes. He was going to accept this new Henry. Take all the good, delete the bad or wild ways, and make for a new and improved Henry. This thought made him feel like he could accomplish his goals and maybe Patrick would forgive him for getting him in this mess. It was a mess. He would ask for forgiveness from his best friend and his mother. He looked over at Bill. Sometimes though it seems your never too old to learn a lesson. But he would try and he smiled at this effort for which he was going to comply with. He saw the two birds reappear. They had not forgotten them. They came back. They found them a place and stood watch. He sensed the hurricane was possibly subsiding some. Good thing.

Henry listened and looked. He thought he heard something out to the north side where the boat had gone missing. He heard a noise like a steady wind sound. Then he heard a siren in the distance far away. Maybe the bridge was opening back up. Maybe he was dreaming it. But the birds returned, they knew, they signaled him. Then he thought he must be losing his mind. Well, it had been a crazy twelve hours for sure. He wondered if he had given them enough information? The car was gone but the bridge was collapsed. Surely, they would investigate that. But no car to be seen though. Did he tell them the south side? Yes, he was sure he had. Should he go out and back up the embankment? No. He should stay put with his injured lot, remain with the crew he told himself. As the sirens got louder the wind sound became steadier. It was a chopper he was sure of it. A helicopter, it had to be. His friend would be rescued. Very soon. He was so relieved he became momentarily delirious with joy.

Patrick lay in his own dream state of unconsciousness from injury, blood loss, and shots of tequila. He felt no pain and came to in his own dream state aboard a train like when he was a little kid. The constant movement and slight motor sound with an occasional whistle when the train slows or stops. He opened his eyes and saw his grandfather sitting across from him. He smiled at him and began talking. We will be there soon Patrick; we will be at the zoo very soon. Are you ready to have a fun day and visit with all the animals? What is your favorite? Patrick just looked at him. He had not seen him in a long time. He looked the same with his long coat, black pants, dark black shoes, and wire rimmed glasses. He smirked that old smirk and tipped his hat. He was a kid again going to the zoo with grandpa. The day would be so much fun. They would be gone all day and would not get back to grandmas until close to midnight. Patrick had not a care right now. He closed his eyes again until it was time to get off the train.

Still sleepy with his eyes closed he heard the whistle really blow and the train came to a complete stop. People started getting loud moving through the train and he opened his eyes. But his grandpa was not there. Sitting across from him was Mr. Sullivan with his mom sitting next to him. Both were asleep. Guys whispered Patrick as he tried to wake them and tell them the train had stopped. Where was his grandpa? Just then the train door to their cabin opened and the train conductor told them it was time. Time to get off the train if this was their destination. He did not know. He looked over at his mom and whispered wake up mom. But she did not move. Nor did Mr. Sullivan. Instead, someone from the army came in dressed in their uniform and said she would be taking it from here. She would get him off the train very quickly. He looked over at them one last time and asked the nice army lady, "Please do not leave them behind, they are my parents."

"I certainly will not. But you are the first to go, okay?"

"Okay."

Back to sleep and out of his dream Patrick remained quiet knowing he was going to be okay. He was going to be rescued and he would see his parents, or his mom, Miss Rachel again.

Henry looked over and saw his bird friends take off to the sky. They went flying away again. The helicopter noise stopped, the whirring subsided slightly, as had the sirens dissipated. He looked both ways to each opening. Which way was best to get Patrick out of here? Out the south on the collapsed tar and up and over them to the highway still intact? Or out the way he had gone up the grassy hill? And did they have a chopper and an ambulance? Each had an obstacle. What was the better of the two?

He looked at Bill and asked him, "Which way do you think is best for Patrick to leave?"

"I think by air and then to the bridge if it still stands."

"It is time guys for the final show, let us be ready." He gathered up any things needed for the day making sure the old man was good. And then he went to Patrick and checked him for the hundredth time tonight but now early morning. "Patrick, they will be here any moment now, probably will load you on a stretcher and pull you out of here and up and over to the bridge. You will get fixed up and see your mom real soon."

"I already saw her," he said.

"You did?" replied Henry.

"Yeah. She fed me and made sure I was ready."

He took Patrick's hand and held it. "That is right. She sure did."

24

Rescue

—Army Medic & Ambulance.

Henry heard the chopper noise get louder as he looked out the north side of the bridge. That is when he saw the chopper go close to the water then displace the water and make waves. He was staring into the windshield of the helicopter and saw the pilot. The pilot gave a thumbs up to him and Henry returned the gesture. Help was here at last. Then the chopper went up.

Two minutes later a woman in an army uniform appeared and scoured their situation. She left briefly and returned a minute later with a rescue stretcher tied to a rope. There would be an air rescue he determined. She maneuvered over to him and saw Patrick on the surfboard and quickly assessed the area. Then she began speaking to Henry and looked over at Bill.

"Are you Henry?"

"Yes, ma'am."

"I am army medic Debra Torres. You and the older gentleman, are you okay?"

"Yes. We are."

"Okay. He goes first by air and then to an ambulance. You

two can walk?"

"Yes, I can. Bill may need assistance."

"Others will come for you. Let me get him out and to the hospital as quick as we can."

"Thank you."

"I will need you to assist me to place him on our stretcher for the airlift."

"Happy to help."

"Perfect."

The army medic and Henry gently moved him by log rolling him side to side. Debra placed the blanket and straps over him, settled him in all the while the chopper floated in the sky just above the bridge. She radioed the chopper pilot after she adjusted herself to the rope and slowly Patrick was moved to the edge of the cement wall and then the two of them glided out over the water from beneath the bridge and up and away, they went. Relief.

Henry looked over at Bill. "I told you they would do an airlift. It is the safest. Best to stay away from this side."

"How did you know? You could not really have known?"

"I was in the army Henry, that is how I know you have done a great job down here."

"Really?" Henry got the chills.

Bill gave him a thumbs up.

"We are next. Can you walk up the hill? It is not too steep. Someone will help you some."

"Yes. I can walk. I walk all the time. Thanks Henry. Are you hurt at all?"

"I do not think so. Maybe overwhelmed is my condition. I do not want to be in charge anymore today. Okay?"

"Right. Okay, you are off duty." The old man laughed. A small joy knowing help was here.

Two ambulance workers appeared and did their assessments of the two remaining victims of the storm. They took their blood pressures and did a quick neurological test of each. Then they walked them up the embankment and onto the road overhead. It was a short walk to the two waiting rescue trucks parked a short distance on the north side of the bridge. A single cop car was also up there. Otherwise, the bridge was empty. Henry could see Patrick was already lowered and rushed into the first truck as it began moving. They were swift. The rescue team put them in the back of the second vehicle and began the process. Then they headed to the hospital as well.

Not once did the rescue team make them feel like they had done something wrong. They treated them with care and caution and were very professional. Henry took note of this. Now was not the time for remarks as to their careless recklessness during hurricane Rebekah. Henry wanted to be just like them, saving lives out on his beloved ocean.

In Patrick's ambulance they scurried around with haste to assess, and place any needed life saving measures in place. What they found was a boy on the edge but still alive. He was pale with a thready pulse and low blood pressure. His eyes responded quickly to light so that was a good sign. They cautiously replaced Henry's blood-soaked bandages with saline soaked gauze and assessed the leg. It was bad and difficult to take in. He must have been in extreme pain and for how long? Oxygen, warm IV fluids, and a dose of epinephrine was administered for blood pressure control. Would he wake? Between the shoulder and the thigh, he must have experienced a living nightmare, they surmised.

Patrick opened his eyes when he heard someone talking in his ear. He could not speak but he heard them. He blinked his eyes when he asked if he was, okay? Did he have pain?

"Henry." He could only muster out his friend's name, nothing else.

The medic told him that he would be going to surgery and could probably see his mother on the way going through the emergency room. She would want to see him. He blinked.

The first rescue ambulance truck arrived and Rachel saw it through the glass doors. She stood and walked near the path the stretcher would take. She waited and it only took a half minute and he was wheeled in with several medics in attendance. As they approached, they slowed down for her to see him. She held his hand and whispered to him.

"Patrick, dear, I am here and I will be waiting for you when you come out of surgery. Do not worry about anything. I love you. You are in good hands." She leaned over and kissed him on the cheek.

And off he went. The next ambulance arrived and the patients were escorted via stretchers as well into the emergency room and rolled into a suite. She saw Henry and they told her to give them ten minutes and then she could come in and sit with him. She went to her seat and called Henry's mother. She told her the roads were not cleared yet as power lines were down and she had no electricity. She might not make it there until much later. Rachel told her she would find out if Henry was to be admitted. Then she would call her with an update.

Once Patrick made it into the surgical suite, the emergency operating room personnel went into high gear. Each of them had their duties and it was very coordinated. He was carefully placed on the operating bed. Xray's were immediately done. The anesthesiologist intubated Patrick after an initial assessment and began anesthesia for the immediate necessity of an operation. Vitals were monitored and the skin was cleansed. He was going to need blood, that was a given, four units were ordered to be given as well as plasma and platelets. A couple of the health care workers gave a knowing glance to one another that signified, Patrick was lucky to be alive. How did he survive for these many hours under a bridge?

The surgery would be lengthy, and the shoulder had to be fixed as well. The team worked quickly, and diligently to save Patrick's life. Even though his blood pressure was very low, he maintained a heart rate compatible with life and the blood would surely help as soon as it was all in. Him being young was to his advantage and that the team worked in perfect harmony added to the patient's success.

Meanwhile, Rachel went in to check on Henry and get the scoop, if he felt like talking. She wondered if she really wanted to know every detail. Also, there was an elderly gentleman with them. Where did he come from? At first Henry was quiet. She told him how grateful she was that he called 911 in the middle of the hurricane and that she was relieved they both would be alright.

For sixty minutes Henry could not stop talking. He told her everything from beginning to end and did not leave out any detail. When he was done, she stood and walked to his bedside and leaned down and gave him a big gentle hug. Then she held his hands and spoke. "You saved my son. You are a hero, Henry."

He looked at her. "I did the best I could. But there will be a new and improved Henry. I promise."

She was not going to scold him. No. She looked at him and smiled, "Henry, you are Patrick's best friend and savior. Someday you will make the best Coast Guardsman they have ever had."

"Thank you, Miss Rachel. Your words mean everything to me. I believe I grew up last night."

"You get some rest. I heard you are staying overnight. I will tell your mother. And I will be here tonight for Patrick. I will visit you later. I am going to say hello to Bill and see that he is okay."

The hospital put Bill in a room for a night of observation right next to his wife. Rachel checked on him while she waited for Patrick's surgery to be finished. It would be a long day but she had nowhere else to be. She grabbed a sandwich from the cafeteria and went back to the waiting room.

Seth arrived and sat next to Rachel and listened to her tell the events which occurred via Henry's take on the ordeal. He was in disbelief and awe. He said a prayer with her as Patrick lay on the operating table. The two conversed and he said he would wait with her until he came out from surgery.

It was a wet and grey day; the sun had not come out yet post hurricane. The television was busy with news covering the damages over the entire area. They sat and listened and looked anxious in their own agony. Rocco arrived much later. Patrick was not out of surgery but the OR team sent out a nurse to convey to them how he was doing.

She informed them of the dislocation of the shoulder with a broken collar bone and upper arm fracture as well. The right thigh was severely damaged, muscles, tendons, and thigh bone. The femur bone was protruding and it was a miracle that he had survived for so long under the bridge. Upon receiving him in the OR he required multiple units of blood. His blood pressure was extremely low, affecting his heart rate but he pulled through that severity. She knew Rachel understood everything being an ICU nurse. Working with the nerves and muscles and skin not to mention the total break of the bone would take more time and a lengthy recovery. It is a miracle she wanted to stress, the surgeon was totally impressed how he pulled through for hours and that his friend apparently pulled him up out of the water and tended to his wounds. She told them approximately three more hours then the surgeon would give them the updated news on the thigh. Would they be here? Rachel said yes, she would be right here until he came out then she would like to see him as soon as possible. No problem she replied. She left and they discussed what they had heard.

Seth asked Rocco if he was staying and he said yes, he would stay with Rachel. Seth said he would call to get the post op condition. It was then that Rachel thought about all the food she had prepared. "I have an idea. I have made a brunch for today but let us have it tomorrow. That way Patrick will be out of surgery, we will know he is okay and he can see our faces. Most likely he will sleep most of tomorrow from the pain medicine and the nurses will take great care of him. The day after is when he will know we are here."

"A wonderful idea Rachel, the condo is close to the hospital." Seth said.

"Yes, I agree." Rocco added.

25

Brunch

At seven pm the surgeon came out and gave Rachel and Rocco the update on Patrick. He sat down with them as he had much to say. They listened attentively and asked questions after he had finished. He answered them and finished by saying, "We are going to close the skin and monitor him very closely. He will be going to the ICU where he will receive great care and, he will be in a medically induced sleep for at least twenty-four hours. Maybe longer if needed. He has been through quite a lot and is not out of the woods yet, but I see a full recovery ahead, though lengthy. I am sure you understand Rachel."

"Yes, yes I do."

"The visiting hours are minimal in the ICU, so rest up as you will be needed after that. We will not extubate him until after that time. If I had to predict I would say around the 48-hour mark, or in two days."

"Okay." Rachel sat taking it all in.

"I spoke with the ICU and you can go in and visit him after they admit him. They will need about an hour. May I suggest you get dinner if you have not already. The time would be around ten o'clock for that visit. Remember he will not be awake."

The surgeon stood as did they. They thanked him for his

work. Rachel and Rocco went to the cafeteria which stayed open until eight pm.

At ten o'clock they walked to the ICU and gave them their names. They were led in and saw him all covered up in blankets and tubes and machines. It was difficult to see him like that and Rachel wept. Rocco held her and hugged her. She was use to all this, just not someone she loved and cared about. He was still. No movement. He looked peaceful. They observed him for about ten minutes. She made sure they had her info. She told them to call her if needed. They gave her a direct number to call for tomorrow and said to come back the following day later in the day. The surgeon and anesthesiologist had given the plan to the unit.

Rocco and Rachel walked out and left the hospital. They would stay at Seth's tonight and have the brunch tomorrow that she had made. Seth was staying with his new girlfriend.

Rocco was not sure how to make Rachel feel better about this whole situation. He just walked with her and put his arm around her shoulder. She leaned on him and appeared to be in a state of shock. Once in the condo she paced around for a bit, then he said, "We should sit on the sofa a while, and just rest, take all this in."

He played some music and poured them a glass of wine from the kitchen. The storm was over. Everyone had survived another hurricane. The boys were safe in the hospital. His grandmother would come back in a few days and things would get back to normal. He was glad to be with Rachel, sitting here made him feel comfortable and needed. He admitted to himself he was falling in love with her. He wondered if she was as well. He would propose a getaway with her tomorrow. She needed sleep and Patrick needed time to rest post op and make it through the first night. The surgeon said this first twenty-four hours was the most crucial.

The night was still and quiet. The hurricane had passed. One could see out the windows again. Around midnight he suggested they get some sleep.

Did she want him to sleep on the couch?

"No," she said. "Come lay with me and hold me. I would like that."

"Alright."

Exhausted they walked into the Bahama Breeze room as Rachel called it. It was nice he thought. Rachel changed and lay down. Seth removed his shirt but stayed clothed and lay down next to her and held her. He covered them up and the pair rested quietly until morning day break. The sun shown in and they opened their eyes having not moved a muscle. Rachel got up to shower and Seth stayed until she finished. Both went to the kitchen to serve Rachel's brunch.

Around ten o'clock Seth and his girlfriend arrived. They brought appetizers and champagne, not to celebrate the hardship but to toast her brunch and that Patrick was out of danger, meaning the surgery was complete.

"I propose a toast to a great mother and her son on his way to healing having survived a tragic night." Seth said it perfect. "By the way Henry's mother is coming by."

"Good. Thanks for calling her. I have enough food for a

small army, for sure."

"We can talk about the night and be thankful," said Seth's girlfriend.

"I checked on the boys and the old man. The old man is being released with his wife today. Henry is being discharged and his mom will bring him by. They will not stay long, but will eat she said." Rocco had called for updates on all involved.

"And tell me what they said about Patrick," asked Rachel.

"Patrick is still asleep from the medicines. He is resting quietly and they will wean him tomorrow morning from the medicine and the ventilator."

"Just like they said." Rachel acknowledged.

"And we will be there to see him. Likely he will be hungry." Rocco added.

"Yes, he will. I will take him a couple sandwiches. He loves these. That is why I made them."

Seth replied, "Another toast then, to Rachel's healing sandwiches and good will."

She could not help it. She had to laugh. She smiled. "Thank you."

Henry and his mom arrived and everyone rose to greet them and give Henry a big hug.

Today was a day of being grateful. Grateful for lives saved, shared happiness and expressions of mutual love.

"Yup, what a difference a day truly makes," responded Henry.

*

Later, the four of them sat around the living room and watched the reports on the television. Then they began talking about the present future and what it held. Plans would need to be made.

Seth proposed that Patrick stay with him in the condo for his rehabilitation. His place is practically next to the hospital. He could set up a room with a special bed and equipment, hire a nurse, and anyone could visit or stay overnight at any time. Rachel thought that was a generous idea and she would think about it. True she lived farther away and she did work. She decided right then it was a great idea. She did not know but maybe intense rehab would be around three months. She remembered she had a friend, another nurse, and she required a whole year staying with her mother after a car accident. Seth told her his student classes were light as many were going abroad in the spring. It became settled that after he left the hospital, if all went well, he would come to Seth's. It was mid-October already; they tried to predict when he might leave the hospital. They agreed on November, give or take. He could care for him from middle of November until early March.

"Good. Let us hope for a good outcome, overall."

"Oh, guys, we have cake. I forgot about the chocolate cake. Everyone gets a piece. I did not give Henry some."

"Take some into the hospital. I bet we run into him there visiting with his friend in a few days."

"Good idea." Rachel served up her cake and they sat at the dining room table eating the divine chocolate on fine white China.

The men did the dishes in the kitchen and struck up a conversation. "I was thinking Seth, that I would like Rachel and I to go to St. Augustine for a trip sometime."

"Oh, yeah. When?"

"Since Patrick will be here with you, I think it would make it easier on her. I have a couple job applicants I would like to interview for the helicopter rescues."

"She is going to love that job. She always wanted to do that. I am happy for her."

"Good." Replied Rocco.

"Sure, go anytime. After Thanksgiving or so, it is all decorated. It is lit up and very festive. You will love it."

"I had heard that. I suppose the first part of December would be good."

"Sounds good."

"That way we will be back for Christmas with Patrick."

"I guess that means I am having Christmas here." Seth liked that idea.

"Maybe we should cook and have them do the dishes." Rocco thought out loud.

"Hey, I like your thinking. We will grill it, whatever it is."

"Hey, sounds like you two are having fun doing the dishes."

"We are working on making your life easier."

"Keep talking then, you two," Seth's girlfriend answered

back.

*

Later that night at Seth's, Rocco and Rachel were staying another night, and Seth returned with his girlfriend to her place, Rocco told her he had a question to ask her. They slipped into the room, in the Bahama Breeze bedroom, and Rocco pulled out his phone.

"Let me show you something." He pulled up what he had been planning. He showed her the pictures. "Would you like to go with me to St. Augustine in December? It has beautiful lights for Christmas and looks magical."

"Really? It does." Rachel looked at all the pictures of lights and decorations set amidst a Florida town on the coast.

"It will be a vacation and one morning of two interviews for the business. I have two candidates over there we can check out."

"Sure. You need more employees, right?"

"Yes, I expect the business to grow to about five or six fulltime employees for the helicopter rescues and two other pilots for the hurricane eyeballs."

"Eyeballs? You funny!"

"You can do the interviews."

"Are you sure?"

"Yes, because you are going to be their boss. I will be the owner, but you are the trainer and boss."

"You really trust me. I love it. Sure, will do. Yes."

"To St. Augustine." Rocco leaned over and kissed her, long and slowly. She returned his gesture and then they held one another. The day ended, tomorrow would begin with the awakening of Patrick. All would be right in the world thought Rachel. And she fell asleep beside her boyfriend and boss.

*

Rachel and Rocco arrived at the hospital after they received a call he would wake up today.

The surgeon and anesthesiologist had seen him at six am and given the orders to stop the induced coma meds and let him awaken. All vital signs were normal and they felt the outcome for extubating should be good. The doctor was worried about infection and would stay on top of that, considering the circumstances of being in the ocean followed by a long period of exposure. But Patrick was young and healthy.

They gave their names again and waited. She told them it would not be much longer.

At 10:30 am, approximately 52 hours after arriving at the hospital and a 14-hour surgery with three surgeons on board and with a whole team in coordination, Patrick was extubated and smiling. He asked a few questions and looked around. The nurses talked with him and answered his questions. He could not move anything but his left hand and arm. He felt weak and wondered what happened. Then he saw his parents. There they were. He was not dreaming, or was he?

"Mom and Dad." Was all he said.

"Patrick. Oh dear. I love you. You are awake. That is wonderful." Each of them stood on a side and looked over him. Joy filled their hearts.

Patrick smiled. It was a small smile. "I am hungry."

"As soon as you can, I have a sandwich for you."

26

Recovery at Seth's

Patrick spent most of November in the hospital healing. Rachel visited most days that she did not work with the rescue helicopter. Seth visited as well and Rocco too. Henry went every day after school, driving his mother's car with her beside him. He was going to be a good driver with this daily experience. Patrick was a happy kid and a tutor came to the hospital to keep his studies going. He had already realized how lucky he was. He knew it that night he spent under the bridge. For his short life he recognized by the look on his friends face it was not good. He prayed to himself. And when his friend offered the tequila, he thought this might be it, and he wanted to feel nothing. The fact that, Bill, the old man said for Henry to give it to him only further told him how dire the situation. But somehow, he held on, he dreamed of train rides with his grandfather back in Ohio. The pleasant thoughts or dreams, carried him through. At times the recovery was painful but nothing like that night. Each day in the afternoon Henry and him did their homework together. Twas like a buddy system. No one ever brought up their misdeed to their relief. They knew they were at fault and had learned the lesson.

One day, a few days before his discharge and before

Thanksgiving, the old man came by to check on him. He brought him peonies in a vase. The flowers were pretty, he had never seen them before, and they smelled nice like perfume. One day he thought he would buy these for his mother. Bill told him he looked much improved. He said Patrick looked like a casualty of war laying there unable to move and no medic in sight. He added, and became very serious, that his friend truly did save his life and deserved a medal for his bravery. Patrick told him he knew he did and would be grateful the rest of his life. Then Bill, got a couple tears leave his eyes and said to him, that Henry saved his life as well because Patrick could not move and he thought quickly to bring him out of his car and over to his makeshift hospital. If he had not, Bill said, he would have likely drowned. He saved us both. What a hero!

Two days before Thanksgiving Patrick was released to Seth's place and would receive rehabilitation at his home with additional visits to the outpatient rehab. Seth would have Thanksgiving and Christmas at his condo this year and he loved it. He set about making all the plans and coordinated with Rachel on the details. December 1st the couple would travel to St. Augustine for five days. Next time they promised to take him or maybe even somewhere else. Where would he like to go they asked?

Patrick answered with Disneyworld when he could walk without crutches or casts.

They promised him as soon as that was possible, maybe in April or May. Cool he thought.

Rachel and Rocco spent time at his house next to the airport. His grandmother had returned with little Johnny, and Xochiquetzal moved in while Rachel worked and visited Patrick. She was not yet in school and Violet knew her language in addition to English. Grandma did not mind at all. It was to help Patrick during his recovery, after that things would go back to normal by late spring. They would help her decorate a Christmas tree and bake cookies. Rachel and Rocco would be leaving in a few days for the trip to St. Augustine.

From the St. Augustine Lighthouse to Spanish bakeries, the big historic fort, beaches and museums, there was plenty to do. Walking tours and the nightlife offered up finishing touches to the day, they would see history unfold in the oldest city in America. First, they needed to settle on a place to stay before every place was booked, then they could finish up the sightseeing touristy sites. And all the Christmas lights would make it extremely special.

"By the time you get back here we will have the tree up, some presents wrapped and cookies made," said Violet. She could see that Rocco and Rachel were drawing closer to one another. This made her smile. He deserved to have a good life with someone special. He worked so hard and did so much for other people. She wanted to see him happy too.

"Violet, can I help you in the kitchen tonight? Maybe you could teach me about the dish you are making." Rachel inquired.

"Sure, come in. Rocco, maybe put a movie on for the kids. They would like that."

The two women worked in the kitchen preparing dinner. Rachel seemed to be adjusted with half her family here, half at Seth's, and her own home over on the beach. Violet told her she was handling it well.

"Time will tell. That is all I need is time. By May 1st all of us should be back to one place and be more settled. We are all blessed that Patrick is recovering well and seems happy. He has many visitors. He has been promised to go to Disneyworld in the late spring, maybe we should all go together."

"What a nice idea. I like that. I will plan on that, you guys come as well."

*

Thanksgiving was at Seth's place and he served it up in excellent taste. He made a turkey and a beef tenderloin on his grill. His girlfriend brought the appetizers, artichoke dips with tomatoes and spinach and fried plantains with salt. While Rachel made sweet potatoes and mashed potatoes, along with Hawaiian rolls and butter. Rocco brought the vegetables, green beans, and broccoli casserole. Violet made two pies, chocolate silk pie and pumpkin, of course.

"Yum, look at that French Silk Pie!" Rachel fussed over the dessert.

"Sweetie, you do not want to know what goes into that pie?"

"I do not? Yes, I do."

"Tell her Violet, tell her how many sticks of butter make

that pie." He was relentless.

Violet raised her eyes. "Too many!"

"Oh, I see, it makes it very creamy and delicious."

The table was set perfectly for eight persons with a place for Patrick at the end. He was wheeled to the table with his leg extension out front. His arm remained in a sling and a neck brace supported his collar bone and neck. He was progressing but still looked like a massive train wreck. But his smile never left his face. He was blessed and he knew it.

Xochi sat next to him and Johnny on the other side with the adults then on each side including Violet, Rocco, Rachel, Seth, and his girlfriend. A full table and plenty of food and blessings to go around. On the television another tropical storm was brewing but this one would take an eastern path and go over on the Atlantic side. At least they would be safe but a prayer was said for the well being of others. Hit or miss, one never knew when it would be their turn down here in Florida. Blessings were said and the feast began. Wine was poured and dishes were passed.

The conversation went from art school, to couples, to St. Augustine, the airport, the beach house, or mansion, and school for the younger set. Studying was easy for Patrick, so he was not behind. He even managed to play a few video games one handed now and then. The other two little ones were still into make believe, tea parties, house, and pretend animals.

Later the pies were passed with small slices given out. Coffee was served and everyone, except the injured boy in the wheelchair and the two little ones assisted with clean up.

"Thank you all for coming. Next up is Christmas!" Seth was already thinking about his favorite holiday and where he would place the tree this year. He looked around.

"Do not worry about that yet," said his girlfriend.

"Wonderful dinner. Thank you so much," said Rachel.

"You two should stay here tonight as you are leaving in a couple days. That way you can see Patrick another day."

Rocco and Rachel looked at one another and replied, "Sure. We would like that."

Violet took the little one's home and Patrick stayed up a while to watch TV. He looked content.

"Honey, just a few more months of therapy and healing and this will all be a memory."

"Yeah. I can handle it. I miss Xochi but she seems to like she is staying with Violet."

"Your mom is right, this will all be a memory, a good memory that you healed rather nicely and life moved forward. Family and people in your life helped you to recover from that horrible storm." Rocco added.

Seth and his girlfriend left. The nurse returned and assisted Patrick to his room for the night. By Christmas Rachel thought Patrick might be out of the wheelchair. She smiled at that thought and gave him a kiss goodnight.

The next day Rachel went to her beach house to pack for the trip to St. Augustine. She stopped once again at the Publix grocery store and bought snacks and drinks for both. A month ago, she was planning for the hurricane, now that was done and she was taking a trip with her boyfriend. It felt special and they had gotten close and comfortable. They would have a chance to be alone without kids or distractions. The idea might of felt like going to paradise crossed her mind. She went through the store and people were still talking about the damage from hurricane Rebekah. She still had the damage, her injured son. But he was healing and her family certainly did not take life for granted. Not one bit.

She had come and went over the last few weeks, staying here, at Seth's, at Rocco's. She was like a woman with too many homes to attend to. In the mornings when she woke, she did not even know where she was, like a traveler feels. That is what she was a traveler. And again, she would be traveling. But with Rocco, her handsome pilot with a winsome smile. How lucky was she? She was very lucky to have met him. Her thoughts lingered on him. They seemed to click handsomely. He was amiable and hardworking, respectful, and she looked up to him as a business owner, a strong man who looked after others. He had a playful side as well, she did too.

Maybe she should buy a special dress to wear. She could do that on her way back to his place, as it was too late to order anything and have it shipped. She would go to the mall and buy something at one of the department stores, shoes too. And new perfume was needed. She found herself feeling flushed and having serious thoughts about him. Could she be in love? She might be. It had been close to three months since they had met and gone out. She could not stop smiling. Her heart filled with joy. Maybe Rocco was the one. Really? Rachel, pull yourself together girlfriend, she told herself. True, she was a mom, but she was a woman and suddenly desire spilled over her.

She packed and left room for a few new purchases. She packed a cooler with items from the store, smiled then packed some more. She loaded up her car, went to the mall, shopped, then drove to Rocco's place. She gave Xochi a very big hug, picking her up and twirling her about. The little girl laughed. Little Johnny wanted a hug too, so she did the same for him. Then Rocco walked in the room and she gazed over at him with new eyes.

27

St. Augustine

Rocco and Rachel departed for St. Augustine before noon as the trip would take around four hours with a stop for a quick lunch. Both dressed casually and looked forward to these five days away. Rachel brought the drinks and Rocco drove his small red car. He had printed out a questionnaire for interviews for Rachel and had her review while he drove. She read it over and circled a few questions and added a couple of her own.

"Thanks. This will come in handy. You are going to be there, right?"

"I will for greeting them and then you will handle the direct interview. I want you to be their boss, and to trust you, to ask you how things will go. Okay?"

"Sure."

"Then when it is complete I will come back in to answer anything not covered and to know I am there for them as well."

"You really are making me an accomplice."

"All the way baby." He laughed.

"Sounds like a plan. I like it."

"This way I really am the boss. I want that boss title."

"You are full of it."

"You bet. I am Rachel's boss. You must obey or else." He teased her.

She laughed.

"Then all the complaints I cannot handle come back to you to fix."

"I think you will make a better partner though if you handle the complaint department."

She stared at him and threw her hands up spilling the questionnaire over the front of the car. "I give up. I think I will hire a department for that at your expense."

"At your expense, since you hired them. Remember? Partners."

They both laughed and enjoyed the ride. Small problems. The big problems were the rescues and rough flights in the eyeballs of storms. Anything else was minor, very minor.

They arrived at a small quaint B&B in the heart of downtown where they could walk to most places. It was brick with a smartly decorated interior. It looked a little like it should be in New Orleans with black wrought iron railings, old world feels inside, and a pleasant woman working the desk. She took their names and drivers licenses, had them sign a paper, and waved her hand over the interior which had a bar and lounge area, and then to the staircase which led to their room. One could see a loft over looking the first floor which had a small fireplace too. Cozy thought Rachel.

"Breakfast is served down here or you can have it brought to your room, your choice. One can be tired out from all the walking you might do," she hinted. "Here's the form for breakfast, leave it down here and we will bring it to you between eight and nine."

"Sounds lovely." Rachel expressed.

"Will you suggest a couple dinner spots that we might like?" Rocco asked.

"Here is a brochure for you. I will circle the best. Are you looking for something special?"

"Good food, good atmosphere. Friendly."

She circled about four spots and handed them the brochure. An assistant helped them with their bags and showed them to their room upstairs. It was spacious with a separate bathroom and living area. A big window showcased the street out front and a smaller window with balcony overlooked a small garden area with a pool and café like setting next to it. It connected to the interior bar and living room.

"However, did you find this place Rocco?"

"Many, many searches. You like it?"

"I love it. I love it already." Rachel looked around. She could stay here a month if she needed.

"Darling, I am pleased that you are pleased."

"Darling?"

"Yes, darling."

"What a surprise. Two things, no make that three, that I like."

"What are those darling?"

"The place is quaint and exquisite. I love it."

"Do go on."

"You called me darling. How sweet."

"Hey, you like that too. And?"

"And, I like you. I like you lots."

"I like you lots, too."

They kissed and embraced one another. Then he pulled her onto the bed and they rolled around like two little lovebirds. They lay there embraced and rested from the short trip. Next up-dinner plans.

Rachel selected a restaurant for the first night. Rocco said he wanted to try a place but he needed to make the reservation. She picked something that had a ship theme with an old time feel. Since the town was established 460 years ago, she wanted to have that pirate feel and maybe seafood. It was close enough to walk, so they strolled around. Some of the lights were on for Xmas, some were not yet lit. It was not quite dark. It had a mystique to it she thought. Many old buildings were now museums or old churches and such. Rocco and Rachel held hands and continued walking to their destination. She chose the Scarlet Rogue which was open until two am. The place was dark, festive, and named after Scarlet from 'Gone With the Wind.' Not exactly old days at sea but the food sounded rogue and fun. Rocco pulled out a map of the town and circled some tourist sites and tried to make a walking path for tomorrow. He figured he was the tour guide. He did want to make this special. He ordered a Cuban sandwich and Rachel ordered a bacon and cheddar grilled cheese. Both ordered a rum and coke. They toasted to themselves and St. Augustine. They would go exploring tomorrow.

She looked around and saw the fireplace, then noticed it had a painting above the mantel. She took a double take, then a sip of her drink. The painting looked familiar. It could not be. No. Must be someone else. Must be a Scarlet, someone named Scarlet. She had Rocco look upon it. She pointed to it. He made a comment like it looks nice; it is a woman sailing a sailboat at night. "She is navigating in rough weather. Oh, she has a bandage over her head with blood on it. But I think it a print."

"Okay, let me have a closer look. Be right back." Rachel went and stood in front of the painting, which was her. It was a print. When did Seth, now teaching at an art school, make prints and sell them? He said he might do this. Maybe it slipped his mind. "Looking good Rachel, hanging on the wall at a place in St. Augustine." She whispered to herself.

"And?"

"It is a print. Nice painting by an artist from the west coast of Florida."

*

The next two days the couple walked everywhere and visited the Castillo de San Marco on Matanzas Bay, an old masonry fort which protected the city. There was so much history the couple could not get all the facts straight, as the city went from the Spanish, to the English, then pirates, and then the confederates, and at last the Americans. They visited the Old Jail, a museum on 167 San Marco Avenue, and many shops in between. They had breakfast served to them two days in a row, the desk lady was correct, room service was perfect.

Rocco saved the fourth day for his surprise, a fancy dinner at an Italian restaurant in the evening after a trip to the St. Augustine Lighthouse. It was a real working Light Station still in operation. It was built in 1871 and the views from the top were incredible. One could see over the whole town and out to sea. Rachel had packed a small picnic for this day trip. The ascended the steps and took a selfie photo up there with the city in the background. Later, they sat near the lighthouse and enjoyed the lunch. They decided to go back to their B&B and sit by the pool, then later get ready for a nice dinner. Tomorrow would be the last day. In the morning would be the two interviews and then they would depart at one o'clock for the trip home. Both were having a nice time. They did check in daily with Patrick and Violet and the two kids.

They went swimming in the heated pool and lounged around. In the water they rested against the edge and began talking about the trip, then talked about themselves and what they wanted in life. They had never really talked about all those things a couple who are dating explore. Things like how many kids did they want, even though she was a mother already. How many did he want? Did he want them? They exchanged ideas about marriage, long term commitments, and what was important to each of them. She liked that they were exploring what the other one felt.

"Life is like a roller coaster; it goes up and comes back down." He said.

"Yes. Enjoy the ride, I guess is the point." Rachel disclosed.

"Together is the key, I believe."

"Together, in love." She looked at him and said, "Rocco, I am in love with you. I know it. I felt it the day before we left."

"I love you, Rachel. I really do."

They kissed. And kissed.

*

Tonight seemed special after the pool talk. Rachel wore her new dress with shoes and splashed perfume here and there. Rocco dressed up in a suit and looked very handsome. They went to the B&B bar and ordered a champagne. A guitar player sang and played light music over near the window.

"I ordered an Uber for tonight. No walking."

They sipped champagne then departed for the Uber which took them to Saint Italian. The hostess placed them in a beautiful booth and they reviewed the menu. Rocco ordered a bottle of red wine, but first a martini called Forever Young. It was a pomegranate and blueberry martini. He had remembered she liked those. She enjoyed this special treatment he was giving her.

The couple in love sipped blue martinis, gazed into each other's eyes, and fell more in love. They seemed to be a perfect match and met during an interview. Imagine that.

Rocco did not know when a perfect time would happen so he just got on with it.

"Rachel, I want to ask you a question."

“You do? Sure. Go ahead.”

“I have a very important question to ask you.”

She looked at him and waited. She sipped her martini and smiled at him. She had no idea.

“My beautiful darling, you are such a delight, a true and kind human being. I just adore you; I love you, and will you marry me?”

She was stunned, surprised, and caught off guard. Her eyes misted. Her mouth trembled. She looked across the table at this most endearing individual and extremely handsome man, who could probably have his pick of many women. He asked her to marry him. Then he pulled out a small present and handed it to her. She took it. She smiled. She was in shock, a good shock.

“Rocco.”

He waited. It was the first time he had ever asked anyone to marry him.

She opened the package and flipped up the lid to reveal a pretty diamond ring. She picked it up and looked at it and put it on. Was this really happening? She looked at him and smiled.

“Yes. I will marry you.”

He came over to her side of the booth and sat next to her and put his head on her shoulder and then turned and kissed her. He was in love and he had known for some time.

*

After dinner and the engagement, they meandered outside to look at all the Christmas lights. It was a glorious sight. It softened the world and made it sparkle like a present. Then he called for the Uber and they returned to the B&B.

Tonight was special. They had not made love since that first time after the shower at her place. Then it had been impulsive, a hunger for each other, now they kissed soft and slow. He took his time with his love, he made tender love to his girl and she returned his desire. Sweet, sweet desire turned into a heated passion neither could put aside.

28

The Interviews

The interviews went according to plan. Both candidates exceeded expectations and both, a female, and a male, were hired on the spot. They would make a great team. Rachel looked forward to working with them. Rocco was proud of his partner and trusted her, she trusted him too. By one o'clock they were driving back home. She wore her ring and gazed at it from time to time. She and Rocco would get married and be a family. She had never been married, nor he. It was a first for both. Many questions entered her mind but she pushed them aside and enjoyed the trip home thinking about St. Augustine. Next time they would bring the kids and take them on a ghost tour atop the lighthouse at midnight if they could stay up for it.

*

A month and a half later …

Tonight was the special dinner at the Fontainebleau in Miami. A prewedding party celebration, or rehearsal dinner, as they traditionally call it. Rachel and Rocco were not traditional and had planned everything themselves. The details would spotlight the couple in a small wedding for friends and family. Tonight, at the Fontainebleau they would share a dinner at the Italian restaurant inside followed by dancing in the LIV nightclub for the old enough patrons. Tomorrow the wedding would take place at Vizcaya in Miami.

They had arrived two days before and sunbathed around the pool then walked the beach. Guests were coming on Friday for the two days stay to celebrate with them. Each of them got ready for tonight and walked to the hotel restaurant. A table for ten awaited them and the party began. Rachel looked stunning in her light floral spaghetti strapped dress and Rocco in his tan linen suit with white shirt. The table accompanied the two of them, Violet, Johnny, Xochi, and Patrick, Seth, and his girlfriend, and two special friends of theirs. Everyone wore a smile in their dressed-up clothes. The table had special flowers and place cards with their names. A violinist played off to the side. Earlier the party had gathered for a brief run through so the kids would know what to do tomorrow. It was quite simple but festive. They had stopped to take pictures in a couple settings before arriving for dinner. Toasts were made to the couple and to Patrick for walking all by himself. He would be the best man but would sit in his chair at the wedding.

After dinner Violet took the kids to their room while the six adults went to the nightclub for dancing. The nightclub had an early Friday crowd but later would fill up and standing room only. They had a reserved table on the second floor with wait help. The atmosphere and music were energizing and upbeat. A smaller dancefloor existed upstairs away from the main floor. At midnight the place had an explosion of confetti trickle through the floors which added to the excitement. From midnight until one o'clock old-time favorites and classics played before the EDM crowd gathered at two o'clock. This party would leave at 1:30 am to get plenty of sleep for tomorrow's wedding day.

One traditional item the couple kept. They would not see each other until the vow ceremony. The wedding would take place at four thirty followed by pictures and the reception would begin at six o'clock. Rocco had a surprise for his bride in between. The reception had been prepared for seventy-five persons including children. Limo service would take persons from the Fontainebleau to the Vizcaya Museum for the event.

The day was already beautiful when Rachel went to get breakfast downstairs. She took it outside and found a table. She was relaxed. In a couple hours she would get ready for the big day. The weather forecast was sunny and bright, no rain, and no humidity. The temperature might reach a high of 76-78 degrees. Perfect she thought. A slight breeze floated through the air. She wanted to stay calm and not worry about a thing. All the plans came through nicely and by Sunday the couple would be a Mr. and Mrs. Oh my what a thought. She had not even thought about that. Sunday they would relax and Monday morning Mr. and Mrs. would leave on their honeymoon. Rocco was surprising her. He liked surprises. And she did not mind; he kept her guessing.

A couple of Rachel's friends helped her get ready in her suite, while Rocco dressed and met up with Patrick and two other friends to ride together. Violet oversaw the little ones. One would drop the rose petals and the other would bring the rings down the aisle. All gathered in different areas and by four o'clock the chairs began to fill with the guests.

There were no bridesmaids or groomsmen, only the pretty flower girl named Xochi and the ring bearer named Johnny. The best man and man to give away the bride were one in the same, Patrick. But he sat in the first row. In charge of the ceremony was a retired Catholic priest honored to be performing the ceremony for his dead brother's son.

And so, it began …

*

A pianist performed the wedding march after playing soft melodic music for thirty minutes while guests sat in the chairs outside along the walkway to the gazebo. The ceremony would take place under the gazebo out by the water. The priest was there, Rocco stood in his white formal jacket with black bow tie and dark pants, finished off with shiny black shoes. His floral boutonnière was peach in color. He looked stunning.

As the wedding march began playing the crowd looked to the aisle waiting for the little flower girl, she wore a peach dress with ruffles in a silk taffeta display. Her long dark hair had soft curls falling from the top of her head and her smile was contagious. She loved her job today. Falling right behind her was Johnny, he wore a navy-blue tuxedo and white shirt with a peach floral flower. He held in his hands the soft pillow of white silk guarding the precious stones of love. He smirked and raised his eyebrows going down the aisle. Why was everyone staring at him he wondered? He handed the pillow to Rocco and he placed it on a chair near the makeshift altar. Both flower girl and ring bearer sat down between Patrick and Violet.

Next up and last was Rachel. She appeared at the beginning of the chairs and stood with Seth, her friend, who was giving her away today. Patrick had the official honor but he remained seated. He had seen her through the tumultuous times down in Florida and they were good friends and coworkers. He walked beside her and brought her to Rocco. She was beautiful and wore a sleeveless off-white ruffled gown that made her look like a goddess of sorts. It flowed and twirled with waves falling from a fountain and its softness lifted her kindness like a flower rising from the ashes of neverland. She had flowers in her hair, which was semi uplifted and exposed her gorgeous pearl earrings. Slightly tanned from the past few days in the sun, her smile added to the spark of love. She looked at Rocco and parted her lips in pure pleasure for this special occasion between them.

The music stopped and the priest began a very short sermon on love and chances in life when two come together. "Where there is life there is harmony of souls. When they unite, they find forgiveness of troubles and blessings doubled through kindness in creating a path all their own for eternity. God sees the love and he pours upon them goodness, a fortune not in money but of purity and genuine faith and honor. Do you Rachel ...”

The couple exchanged their vows to one another.

“Do you Rocco ...”

Upon the completion of vows and ring placements, “You may now kiss the bride.”

The couple kissed and then turned to the small crowd of gatherers. The music started up and down the aisle they went, followed by the ring bearer and flower girl. Those in attendance cried a couple tears of joy and smiled as they departed to an awaiting horse drawn carriage off to the side. Rocco had a surprise for his bride and there it was in front of them. He held her hand as she stepped up to the carriage. How romantic!

Once in the carriage the horses took off and the master drove the carriage around the estate. Rocco opened small bottles of champagne inside and the two privately toasted to being Mr. and Mrs. Rocco Sullivan. Then they really kissed as the escape vehicle traveled around the gardens, the endless gardens, and fountains. How could Rachel fall anymore in love? She loved this man. He had surprised her and everyone. Rocco felt on top of the world and he had the biggest blessing of all, his love right beside him. He felt miraculous!

Pictures. Champagne. Dinner. Cake. Dancing. Celebrating this new love coastal style.

After a trip through wonderland and the gardens the couple returned and were greeted with applause and champagne toasts. The photographer had them pose against the stone railing and he took pictures seaside. The bride and groom, the flower girl, the ringbearer, the priest, and Patrick, best man and giver of the bride stood in various positions for the photographer while guests found their seats at tables and by six o'clock waiters were taking orders for the dinner dining outside. Several toasts were made, champagne poured and the reception was in order. Music played from a small band with piano and a singer performed numbers. As the sun set, the dinner was served, and joy overflowed at the waters edge outside the historic residence now named Vizcaya. While guests dined the singer sang classic tunes and a few edgy jazz numbers most recognized as love tunes.

Once dinner was complete guests began dancing on the dance floor. Others mingled and talked, gave their blessings personally to the couple, and everyone rejoiced upon the evening.

Then it was time for cake cutting near the head table. Simple and elegant the cake was all by itself. No fuss, just slices of sweet surrender. More pictures captured the bites of cake slipping into the lovers' mouths and the waiters offered each table slices for themselves.

At the main table Seth asked the couple where they were headed for the honeymoon. "It is a surprise," spoke Rocco. He looked at Rachel.

She responded, "I love his surprises. The carriage today was fabulous. He never told me."

"Nice touch there Rocco." Seth admitted.

"I am sure it will be bliss wherever you go. Many

blessings." Seth's girlfriend said.

"Thank you both. And thank you for filling in for Patrick with the walk down the aisle."

"You are very welcome. I wish you a wonderful honeymoon."

"Time for the traditional couple's dance," announced the band.

Rachel and Rocco made their way to the dance floor with all eyes on them. A special song known only to them played on and on as they twirled slowly, together around the floor. When it finished, they kissed and gave others a chance to spin around under the stars on this evening in January by the sea. They both relaxed and enjoyed their wedding. It was possible to enjoy and be there for each other, yourself, and not to entertain a crowd. Her mother would have been proud of her on this blessed evening. They could not make it as they were elderly now and unable to travel. Rocco's were dead. They had their small group and the world turned despite these misgivings. Around nine thirty the married couple said their goodbyes and thanks for coming words. Off they departed to a waiting limo back to the hotel. The guests waved them off after a beautiful wedding day and evening.

29

The Requisition for a Painting

Prequel for the Fifth Novel in Series

A large yacht sailed out of the Caribbean waters. She had been over to Europe cruising around during the hurricane in the gulf. Now she was headed home or her home away from home and cruised up the western coast of Florida. Out from shore but still close to see the shore. The gentleman who owned the yacht was getting some morning sun on the upper deck before lunch. He had a crew to attend to every need aboard, and he had guests with him for a couple weeks.

This afternoon after lunch he was set up for a game of chess with another player. The owner had played in his younger years but had not touched the game since yesterday, so he was in essence relearning a long-forgotten skill. No matter, this did not bother him. He was always game. He liked learning new skills, keeping abreast of new ideas. First and foremost, he was a business man, not a player, wealthy beyond, and he liked to get the bad guys from time to time.

This gentleman was married and had children who had graduated college and needed careers. So yesterday he bought some businesses and he planned on putting them in charge with his help. They had said, yes, dad, sure we will run something for you. He was pleased with himself. His wife was joining him in a few days as she went to attend to her mother who was ill. He missed her already.

"Sir, let me put some sunscreen on your back." Said one of his attendant's.

"Sure. Is it red already? I have only just switched sides you know." He let the girls tell him what to do. It was their job to look after him. He did not mind at all.

"We have come to join you up here," said one of his guests.

One of the couples staying with them arrived to sunbathe with him. Good he thought I have some company. They chatted and the server brought them drinks. After a while he turned back over and sat up. He pushed up the umbrella to cover himself and just soak in the atmosphere.

"Are you enjoying the sailing out here?" he asked them.

"It is exquisite, sir. The ship is beyond beautiful. We are so thankful that you asked us to be a part of your voyage in the gulf."

"Great. After lunch we are having a game of chess inside. Please join us, there will be several tables. Do you play?"

"We do. That would be nice."

"And tonight, dinner will be in the formal dining area and I have a pianist playing for us. You might want to even dance some."

"Yes, I will be sure to dress up for the occasion," the woman added.

"I will as well, save me a dance," he said.

"Lunch is served," announced the waiter. He waved his hand towards the outside dining area under an umbrella tarp for shade. Music played via speakers and the guests were treated to full service.

He sat down at his spot and noticed his cell phone ringing. He picked it up and it was one of his daughters. "Hello honey, how are you? Are you coming tonight? I have great news to tell you."

"Yes, dad, I will be there. I am bringing a date. You good with that?"

"Of course, any date, any time." He was being courteous, of course, it mattered but he was in a good mood.

"Great, see you tonight. The helicopter is picking me up at five and I will see you at six for drinks and dinner."

"Perfect. How about your sister?"

"She will not make it until tomorrow, but Levi is coming with us."

"Okay, great, two out of three works for me."

"And mom is coming the day after; I spoke with her a few minutes ago."

"We have guests, so dress up."

Lunch was lobster rolls and pineapple slaw. White wine and lemonade were offered. Lunch was followed by tea and cookies, banana pudding too. It was a perfect day, a soft breeze was blowing, the ship cruised slowly and the views were magnificent. A perfect day at sea.

The group finished lunch and went to the inside area or lounge area for a game of chess. It would be a friendly game, or learning game as he was still getting the rules back into play. "You know chess became part of the Olympics in 1924."

"I did not know that."

"In Paris, of course."

"Okay let us have at this. Give it a good try."

He had an instruction book to refer to if needed. They played for a couple hours casually before retiring the board. No checkmates. Mostly, they talked and helped each other learn the game. "We will just have to keep at this, I suspect."

He received a call and walked away to attain some privacy. He had been waiting for this for a few hours. "I am so glad you called."

"What can I help you with sir?"

"I have been told that you are a remarkable painter. The word is out."

"Really? I have sold a few paintings but I did not think anyone had my name."

"I am a friend of Scarlet's. But she did not tell me. It was a student of yours who was selling a painting online and I saw it. Then I saw your work."

"Yes, go on."

"You sold a painting to a restaurant manager of mine. We do business together. He loves the painting. He put it above his hearth, the fireplace in the main dining room."

"Really? Wonderful."

"It appears you are good at portraits, possibly."

"I have done a couple of those."

"I would like to commission a painting of my daughter's Oliver Chestnut."

"Oliver Chestnut."

"Yes, Oliver Chestnut III."

"The third?"

"Yes, he is the third Springer Spaniel in line. And I just think he qualifies for a formal portrait, don't you?"

"For sure. Do you want it from a picture or a sitting, or both?"

"I believe both, for coloring, and accuracy."

"Sure. When would you like this painting to be finished or thereabouts?"

"I want to give it to her for her birthday, this November."

"I love that. That is plenty of time since it is March. Of course, I can do that. Now let us talk price."

"No worries about price, but give me an estimate."

"Estimate?"

He paused.

"What size would you like?"

"Yes, size matters."

"Large, like lifelike or bigger."

"Okay, let us do seven foot high. Anything bigger is museum quality."

"How much?"

"I would say, approximately three months work, off and on, the price will be ninety thousand."

"Perfect. I look forward to it. I will let you know when we are in town, which will be very soon."

"I will need four or five photos and one live sit in. Then I will capture his demeanor and atmosphere around people."

"She will love it, and I will too."

"Thank you for your business. See you soon."

He hung up and thought this would be the best surprise for his daughter. Maybe he should do something for his wife. What did she need or want? He did not know. Then again, he had just bought her something yesterday. Maybe he would ask her later this week.

After the chess game he headed for the deck to walk, then his room for a quick nap and a shower for dinner tonight. He would likely walk around the deck for some exercise too. He would be dancing tonight. The ship was fun when sailing with the crew and family and friends. He was glad he bought it.

Yesterday he bought three companies and tonight he would tell his daughter and son which ones were going to be their responsibility. She and he had raised three good kids who wanted to help. Many times, you heard the opposite but not this group. He was blessed for that. So, he treated them well. He walked around the deck four times and then he hit the shower, followed by a short nap. He was fit and in the prime of his life. Life had turned out pretty good for him and he was thankful. He had developed a social media site and sold it for a huge profit. That was years ago and now he bought companies, played with them, sold them, or kept them. It was kind of like chess. What was next?

He showered. He napped. He dressed. He went down to the lounge area for a drink before dinner. Tonight, he felt like a Manhattan. He ordered a Manhattan with a cherry. He sipped his cocktail and waited for his son and daughter and date and other guests to join him. He called his wife while he waited. She missed him too and would be joining him the day after tomorrow. Her mother was ill and deteriorating rapidly. She had to place her in a home as she could not care for herself any longer. She could not really come on the boat, as she might wonder off and fall into the ocean she told him. He agreed. He was sorry. Maybe there was something they could figure out. They would discuss this in person. They said their goodbyes. They were still in love. He was not a player like some very rich men. He was a family man, true and true.

His daughter and date and son arrived before the other guests and he was glad about this. He wanted to tell them the good news. They ordered a drink and sat with their dad. They were so happy to see him. He looked well and very happy.

"I had a good day playing chess, tanning myself and eating lobster on deck."

"Did you win or checkmate at chess?"

"No, we are both relearning the game. Maybe by the end of the week we will have a battle of the minds."

"What did you want to tell us dad?"

"Oh yes. Listen up, I bought three companies and a vineyard. The vineyard is for your mother, do not tell her. Okay?"

"Okay, we will not. Oh my god she will love it. She will want to move there pronto. I just know it. She has wanted to work one for years."

"I know."

"And."

"I bought an AI company, a clothing startup, and a battery

company for electric vehicles."

Their eyes were amazed. The expressions were priceless. Would there be a fight?

"You can either pick or I assign. Your choice."

"I will take the AI company," said his daughter.

And his son said, "I will take the battery company." He nodded at him. He knew he would pick that.

"Then, your sister gets the fashion start up. I know she would pick that anyway."

"And mother gets the vineyard." His son and daughter and date smiled at him.

"Let us go to dinner and discuss further."

They joined the other guests and sat down at a table and were waited on by his staff. Tonight was steak and scallops with potatoes and green beans accompanied by a good cabernet wine and a cheesecake for dessert. The pianist played beautiful music and sang a couple numbers. Happy people happy times all aboard the yacht out to sea sailing the warm waters off the west coast of Florida.

*

Rachel and Rocco had a relaxing day poolside, a workout, and a trip to the spa. The next day they prepared to leave and packed their luggage. She still did not know where he was taking her.

Until he showed her the ticket.

30

The Honeymooners

"Bahamas," she exclaimed. "How exciting. I love it there."

"You do?"

"Yes, I went there a long time ago with a friend, a coworker from the first hospital I worked at. It was called Paradise Island."

"Oh, baby, that no longer exists."

"It doesn't?"

"No. Something else replaced it."

"No worries. This will be just as beautiful, I am sure."

They found their seats on the plane in first class. Rocco made sure this trip would be memorable. They settled in and the flight attendant brought them a cocktail and snack.

"Darling, I thought the wedding went perfectly, do you?"

"Absolutely perfect. I enjoyed myself and remember everything. I believe our guests loved it as well."

"And what about the surprise?"

"I loved that too. Simple, romantic and I think you put a spell over me since that ride."

"A spell? Yeah, that is me, the spell maker. Now you are in one for the rest of your life. There is no escape, from me or the spells." He laughed.

"Darn, I am trapped in a romantic spell for the rest of my

life. I do not believe I wish to ever escape. It sounds like a wonderful life, you and me, and the whole wonderful world."

"If you get mad at me, I will just have to add a spell and undo the madness."

"Mr. Charming, let them loose. I am game for your charm's sweetie." She smiled. The honeymoon was off to a great start.

The wedded couple checked in to the hotel resort amidst tall palm trees and lush tropical florals of bright orange hibiscus and azalea-colored azaleas. Large pillars stroked the front entrance and a two-story lobby welcomed them into their honeymoon place. Large terra cotta tiles swept the floor and the grandness emerged and entranced them into another world. They were greeted by welcomes and a glass of champagne. The bellman took their luggage and after a quick stop at the desk laden with flowers and smiles they were briskly walked away to a golf cart that drove them to their suite near the ocean. Each suite was its own home in paradise.

"So private, honey."

"You like?"

"Love it already."

They walked to the door with their champagne and dreams. The bellman opened the door and escorted them in and placed their luggage near the staircase. Rachel took it all in and turned completely around to capture the interior. A staircase led to a second floor with a sweeping loft view of the ocean and the lower level. Rocco handed him some bills and he left them to explore. They walked to the back towards the large double story window and glass door opening.

"Breathtaking, I would say."

"Ginormous and stunning, I will add."

Once in the back they turned around and saw a dining room, kitchen, and sitting area. A small library was off to the side with a fireplace and candles. Then they opened the glass doors and stepped outside onto a patio and walkway right to the ocean. It was them and the ocean. They were right on the beach and viewed the gentle waves. The ocean was calm today and would soon be like glass as the day ended.

They walked back in and Rocco carried their luggage upstairs and Rachel followed. The upper loft had a seating area and views out the double story windows overlooking the ocean and outdoor palms. Sunsets would not be a problem this week. Their suite faced west in the Caribbean. There were two bedrooms and they selected the master. Now this was a Bahama Breeze room Rachel said. The beautiful floral-patterned bedspread and four poster bed sure looked inviting. It was white and the windows had white shudders on the interior adding a nice touch of island old-world charm. Real live flowers adorned the high-top dresser. There were birds of paradise and gladiolus and other flowers she had no idea what they were.

"Come see in here, Rachel." Rocco had walked into the bathroom. It was like a day at the spa. His and her separate vanities, separate toilets, a huge shower, and a bathing tub right in the center of the room. His and her beautiful terry robes lay over the tub and a swan décor from a towel between them.

"We are not going to want to leave. Ever." She spoke.

"Lots of pampering for us, all week long, honey. I love you and I get to love you and pamper you every day."

They kissed and smiled at one another.

"I do not know if you know this about me but I like to unpack right away, then it is done."

"I am on your ship darling."

"Sweetie, always call me that, okay?"

"Sure. But maybe I will call you my queen or something grander from time to time."

"I am pretty sure I might be calling you something else by midweek."

"Oh yeah. What might that be?" He smirked at her.

"Ah, maybe something like, hey lover."

*

The first night they dressed casual in shorts n polo shirt for Rocco and a simple navy cotton dress and flip flops for Rachel. They walked the path which led to one of the restaurants and were seated. They watched the sunset of peach hues in the sky reflected onto the glass like water from their table and ordered dinner. Both ordered a cheeseburger and a pina colada with dark rum. They discussed the week and what activities did both want to do. They concluded on walks on the beach, a boat ride, dancing, a festive night by the islanders, a bike ride, a casino night, a couple nights in the suite watching the sunset, and loving each other most every night. He added he would serve her breakfast in bed a couple mornings. Sounds delicious she said.

The next morning, he brought her breakfast in bed like he promised. Then they put swimsuits on and went for a walk on the beach right from their back door. This was followed by a boat ride from the dock nearby. Later they lazed by the pool and took in an hour of sun. Tonight, would be dancing not far from the hotel lobby. They could walk and so they did. Slow songs, fast paced and some reggae rocked their souls on the dance floor. The place was packed. Seemed everyone had this idea tonight.

After a while Rocco asked her what she wanted to take back to the suite. He got them both a drink and they strolled the path through the jungle like setting lit up with lights back to their suite. They held hands and heard a couple parrots cawing in the night. Back in their suite Rocco set the drinks down in the kitchen and turned the music on low and went to his bride. Looking out the big picture two story window the ocean was lit up. He held her and embraced her body, then turned her to kiss her sweet lips. Both closed their eyes and dreamily swept up in longing and desire became anchored to one another. He undressed her as she did him and two bodies became one in a magical moment of time.

He made them a snack and poured two drinks over ice from the bar cart. "I think we need to stay up a while and watch the moon descend over the ocean tonight."

"Good idea." She followed him upstairs to the Bahamian suite.

The couple sipped and snacked on crackers and cheese and grapes and nuts.

Around one in the morning the full moon slipped into their view but Rocco was now on top of Rachel in a sensuous pose and pushing for control while Rachel ached within. Desire consumed them both as they made passionate love to one another. They called out love tenders to one another by name and released all inhibitions. This union filled them to the core and a release was imminent. Their love for one another made this moment unique to them. The world did not matter and time stopped until they were finished and laid on their backs. When their senses returned, they looked over at the moon and then each other. The tenderest of 'I love you' was shared between them.

*

Morning came they rode bikes around the place and beyond. A cute little café near the pool was where they had lunch. They talked about this and that and Rocco brought up the subject of a home. "Where shall we live my darling?"

She perked up and said, "I have no idea. Do you?"

"I have been thinking about it."

"We could live in the beach house, rather mansion, for a while. My friend is gone for two years."

"Yes, I know. But after that we should find us a home. The airport house is good but I think we will need a bigger place with a neighborhood for the kids."

"You are so right. Kids need friends to ride bikes with, catch the school bus, etc."

"We should look at neighborhoods."

"And close to the airport for work. That will make it easy for both of us."

"Tonight is the big toga party. You up for that?"

"Yes. Sounds like a blast."

"The performers I am told do a fantastic job as we sit there in our makeshift sheets pretending to be Romans." He laughed.

"I wonder if they give us a crown of leaves?"

"I believe they do Cleopatra." He smirked at her.

"Is that so Julius Cesar?"

"And, so it goes, we go as two greats tonight. However, will we conquer the world?"

"Everyone will bow down to us and part as we pass by."

"To Cesar."

"To Cleopatra, the most beautiful woman on earth, dear."

*

Cleopatra and Julius Cesar watched a fire and ice show on stage. The performance was mesmerizing with the fire, and a sculptor with quick skills made a dragon in front of them. The crowd was wowed. They dined on lobster and crabmeat, a spicy island carrot soup, and pumpernickel bread with a special butter spread. Chocolate lava cake was presented for dessert. They mingled with the others at their table and enjoyed this festive event making toasts to the best toga attire. Rocco was relaxed and he knew Rachel was having a wonderful time as she laughed and smiled at him, kissing him periodically. She and him had made their wedding unique and special and he had surprised her with the best honeymoon money could buy he thought.

They slept in the next day and did not move out of bed until around eleven in the morning. This day would be a total lounge day with tonight a hand at the casino. Plenty of time to relax. They walked out the back door and put two chairs right on the beach. Rachel made sandwiches and brought them out to them both. They sat and ate and drank a beer. Tomorrow they would return home. And see the kids. Yes, they had missed them but not too much. This was their time alone and they knew it. Both fell asleep in the lounge chairs on their private beach before them. It was not until the tide rolled up and hit their toes they woke up. They were shaded so no worries about a sunburn, and they both had a good tan anyways after a week in paradise.

Casino night was fun but the feeling came over them, tomorrow they were leaving. One last night to revel in paradise and this special suite. They did not waste the moment nor the night.

*

"What did you like best darling, besides me?" He asked her on the plane.

"The sunsets, honey."

"Why the sunsets?"

"They tell me tomorrow is coming."

"Sweet."

THE END